THE ALIBI

Copyright 2002 by
Dennie Kuhn
and
JumpNJupiter
All rights reserved.

Electronic and soft cover print versions
Published by JumpNJupiter

Original Art Work by
David Howard

ISBN: 0-9719362-1-8

Printed in the United States of America

The Alibi

By

Dennie Kuhn

Despite astounding support from everyone close to me, *The Alibi* is for my husband, Martin, and my sister, Sarah. Their confidence in me is a perpetual inspiration.

Chapter One

The cop was getting ticked. For the second time she snapped, "License and registration, please, sir!" Stern green eyes held his.

Riley knew he should answer. He should have answered the last five increasingly hostile queries, but for some reason, he couldn't tighten his slack jaw. His body felt drained and weak, and he couldn't remember what he had been doing a few minutes ago, or even how the cop had come to the window of his Suburban. Had he rolled it down to talk to her?

The blonde cop leaned forward and sampled Riley's air with a crimson nose. He knew she smelled no booze; in fact, he could smell *her* last cappuccino, although frigid air was filling the cab of the truck. "Hmm! Maybe I should call an ambulance, sir. I'll be right back." Her softened tone was cheering.

Riley squeezed his eyes shut as she returned to her patrol car. The insides of his eyelids were grassy, but it felt good to close them against the dazzling sun. What time was it, anyway? It seemed too bright for early morning. Shivering a bit, he tried flexing his fingers, and, finding that they obeyed his commands, he lifted them experimentally. Same old hands, same old fingers—except for one thing. His wedding band was gone. Its tan line was a pallid scar.

Riley wiggled his toes and reflected on the past night and

morning. Was it possible that he had driven around for hours, in a daze, not caring where he ended up, hardly aware even that he was driving? He'd only wanted to escape Alice and their argument, and it was disconcerting to find his memory so unreliable.

The cop was watching him. Riley could feel her watching him from her patrol car, the familiar sensation of eyes on the back of his neck reminiscent of those years spent under his father's constant, invisible gaze. Privacy had been a commodity in that house, with Daddy dear the sole shareholder. After the first time, Riley had learned to be far more aware, and to trust his instincts. Once he'd realized the eyes were there, it became even more impossible for him to relax, but he had been too afraid of his father to confront him. Eyes in his closet, eyes through the keyhole, eyes on him as he walked to school or took a shower or as he fell asleep. Riley always knew when his father—or anyone else—was watching him.

He always knew, and he knew right now.

Riley tried to turn his head around to meet her gaze—it moved a little, but it was easier to angle his eyes up toward the rear-view mirror. To his surprise, the cop wasn't watching him; she was gazing into a computer screen and talking into her radio. Her face glowed computer-screen-green. He tried again to move his head and managed to wobble it around. There was no one else in sight. Shock plays games with your mind, Riley decided, keeping an eye on the cop, but his heart skipped a beat.

Strength was returning steadily now, and the cobwebs were dissipating. A hot cup of coffee would probably help! Also his stomach was complaining bitterly and loudly. Maybe he wouldn't need that ambulance after all.

The cop left her car with such suddenness that Riley lost sight of her for a few moments. "Hello?" he croaked, meaning to call, and his throat burned like he'd just gotten his tonsils out. Swallowing painfully, he tried again.

The cop appeared about four feet from the truck, and a little back from his window. Her gun was drawn and she had it aimed steadily at his head. "Sir, I need you to step out of your vehicle, please," she said, and the softness he'd heard before had grown a hard shell.

"I don't know if I can," Riley whispered. "Can you help me?" She hesitated. Why did she want him out of the truck anyway? Couldn't she see he was sick or something?

"Sir, do your best to get out, right now."

Riley swallowed his irritation. It was best to do what the cop ordered and straighten it out afterward. Besides, she was very intimidating. "Okay." He put his hand on the door handle. The big door swung open.

"Okay, now, take it easy, sir."

"What is this about?" he asked. Both legs were cooperating, but he was having trouble with his hips. His feet dangled absurdly from the Suburban.

"We'll talk about it just as soon as you're clear of your vehicle, sir. Try grabbing the doorframe and pulling yourself out."

He did so, now suspecting that something was seriously amiss—and there was much more his unreliable memory was neglecting to share. It took monumental effort to pull his body out of the truck, and when he finally managed, his knees buckled and Riley found himself face-down in the snowy, muddy ditch. Frozen gravel cut into his cheek.

"Um," he said, trying to maintain at least an iota of dignity.

The cop wasn't concerned with his dignity; she bolted forward and stood over him. She wore exceptionally shiny black boots with bright yellow laces. The sound of metal on metal seemed to confirm the severity, if not the reality, of the situation. "Are you cuffing me?" Riley gasped, disbelief washing over him in an electric wave. Cold steel bit into his wrists and he heard her grunt as she shifted position, her boots slipping in the slush. His shoulders were seized, and, to his astonishment, he was hauled out of the ditch with startling strength. She propped him up against the Suburban like a surfboard and looked into his eyes.

But the cop's face had changed! Her face had paled and

widened; her nose and lips were sunk into the flesh. The fingers clamped onto his shoulders were long and wet and grey. Riley gasped and tried to pull away, but his muscles had returned to their liquid state. Fear invaded his every cell as the thing tightened its grip and lifted him a few inches off the ground.

Recognition swam up from the depths of memory like a forgotten nightmare. The black, soulless eyes flung his horrorstruck face back at him. The eyes! The eyes gazed into his mind!

The thing opened its mouth to speak.

"Riley Aisling," it said, the shaky female voice issuing forth from the slit horribly incongruous, "you're under arrest for the murder of your wife, Alice Aisling."

The rest was lost in a whirlpool of sirens and eyes and sex and dread.

Chapter Two

He awoke lying on his right side with a pillow propped under his head to keep his neck straight. The air was cold and dry; it had a medicinal flavor and though light was limited, Riley could see other beds flanking his own.

Remaining motionless, Riley waited for his eyes to adjust and listened for other occupants; there were none. He could hear only his own heart and lungs and the omnipresent buzz of the fluorescent hallway light. What had happened? Where was he? He searched his memory.

At first, nothing, a barren desert... a few tumbleweeds rolled lazily through... and then...

A few

Drops

Of water.

Alice.

Was.

Dead.

The fight, the drive, the cop...

It all came back in a horrific rush, Alice was dead, the fight, the drive the cop...

You're under arrest for the murder of your wife, Alice Aisling...

With a tiny nudge, the floodgates creaked open, and now

Riley found himself without the strength to push them shut against a torrent of memories. He remembered the last night he and Alice had shared; he remembered the first time they'd made love. He had memories of their first date and their first fight, he remembered Alice, looking pale and lost and lovely at his father's funeral. He recalled holding Junie's new baby, a warm bundle who giggled up at him and drooled on his wristwatch.

Awash in this torrent, Riley struggled to keep afloat, and noticed as he did that other things were awash with him. Alice bobbed a few feet away; there was a jagged hole in the side of her skull and the cold water hurried in. *I'm too good for you and I don't love you!* The cop-thing who had arrested him was floating nearby too, its blonde hair wet against the hideous grey face. It hissed and started paddling toward him.

No! He had to get those floodgates closed and escape before he drowned or was drowned. Summoning all his strength, he pushed desperately at the obstinate gates, his feet churning against the water like fleshy propellers.

Even as the cop-thing splashed closer and closer, something more terrible approached, unseen. He could sense a giant roiling creature pressing against the gates on the other side... Frantic now, Riley pushed with all his might, crying out as the gates resisted a moment longer, then groaned shut. The monstrous memory on the other side howled and pounded at the gates with a dozen terrible tentacles, then splashed away and faded into the darkness.

Riley sat up sobbing, his face drenched with tears and sweat, and saw a figure standing in one corner.

"Who are you?"

The figure took a few steps out of the corner and put his hand out to flick a light switch. Fluorescent light flooded the room, and Riley once again waited for his eyes to adjust before he could see a man about his own age. The man was wearing a lab coat and had blond hair. "I'm Doctor Walker. You're in a prison medical facility. Someone's been waiting to speak with you."

Doctor Walker opened the door of the infirmary a crack and said something to someone in the hallway. Then the door opened all the way and a woman entered.

"I'm the Chief of Police, Mr. Aisling. My name's Sarah Janis. Now that you're conscious, I just wanted to be sure you're aware of your rights. The arresting officer said she didn't have a chance to Mirandize you before you passed out. Do you feel up to answering some questions?"

Riley took a deep breath.

The cops were swarming Junie's house, buzzing angrily around the crime scene, flitting around the grid, social and efficient. They collected evidence as though it were pollen—laboriously, meticulously, and hungrily. Detective Hilde Casey often wished she had never been promoted, for though she was still a part of the hive, she was also forever in flight outside of it, not that the sensation was unfamiliar. She had worked twice as hard as any man, and sacrificed twice as much to advance in the force. She never expected to feel empty and depressed upon her promotion to detective, but here it was—a year later and no happiness in sight.

The victim's sister, Junie, sat in the kitchen, drinking coffee laced with tears. Casey thought of her own sister, the cop who had arrested Riley Aisling, who she worried about every day, and seated herself at the table. "I'm Detective Casey. Sorry you had to walk in on this."

"Thank you. But it was only a matter of time."

How interesting. "What do you mean by that?"

Junie's lip curled a bit at this; it displayed her canines and was extraordinary to watch. "My sister never grew up, Detective. She was used to getting what she wanted, from anybody. If that meant drugs, or sex, or money, or anything else, she got it. Half the time, though, she didn't *know* what she wanted. She was dangerously impulsive. It was bound to catch up with her."

Casey nodded. "What about her husband?"

A shake of the head; a long blink. "Riley thrives on routine and comfort. He was an impulsive acquisition—he's something she didn't want anymore."

Hilde fell silent a moment. Her own relationship with the opposite sex was strained, and not only because she worked eighty-four hours a week. She just couldn't help but feel that when there was a man in her life, she had acquired a new tedious and nauseating chore, like promising to care for a neighbor's diarrheic mutt, and it was always a relief when the neighbor returned from vacation. She made it crystal clear to any man she became involved with: Sex was all she expected from a relationship; isn't that what they both wanted anyway? "Do you think he killed her?"

Junie lit a cigarette and unconsciously tapped the tip on the rim of her empty coffee cup. "No. Alice was infuriating, and she was unfaithful and mean, but Riley's a gentle guy. I can't see him... doing that to her. He loved her very much."

Love hurts. Sometimes it kills. "Thank you for talking with me. Can I give you my card? Call anytime, okay? By the way, do you know who that is on the answering machine?"

Junie shrugged and dragged off her cigarette. "Alice had men. That's one of them."

Hilde smiled. *Had men.* Interesting choice of words, like *had horses* or *had cars*. Finding out where that phone call came from would be no problem—they'd just check the phone records—but if the call originated from a public phone, the caller's identity would be more difficult to ascertain. She said, "Uh-huh. Did her husband know she was unfaithful?"

"He knew. Riley... just didn't know how to do anything about it." Junie's azure eyes were wistful. Ah. Perhaps she was envious of one particular possession? Junie was pretty, but not a knockout like her sister, and Hilde had to wonder how far sibling rivalry could push a person.

"I'm sorry I have to ask you this, but where were you this morning, between 3:30 and 4:30 A.M.?"

"I was at a party."

"Witnesses?"

"About twenty." She smiled wanly. "It was a really good party, and my mom took the kid."

Hilde nodded, happy to have eliminated a suspect already. "I'll need the names of your witnesses, and, for the ones you remember, their phone numbers. Give them to that officer over there, okay? I'm heading back to the station. Remember, call any time."

Riley Aisling was smaller than Hilde expected, since she had inspected the victim's cracked skull and her devastated face bones, but he was still bigger than his dead wife. Hilde had met many killers, perhaps a dozen in her ten years on the force, but as she imagined that mask whispering into the ear of a dying woman as he pulled the cord tight around her throat, Hilde settled without difficulty into her bad cop routine.

"So why'd you do it, huh?" she asked as she turned the chair around, swung a leg over it, and leaned on its back. She always sat backward in chairs like this one; she couldn't help it. It was a cop thing.

Aisling's mask warmed, and the eyes met hers. "I didn't do anything," he said in a tiny shocked voice.

"Give me a break, pal!" Hilde snorted. "You're in this wonderland because there is evidence to support an arrest, understand? I saw what you did to her. I just want to know why."

"No," Aisling said in the same tiny voice. "We had a fight, I left, and I drove away…"

"Then what?"

"I can't remember."

Hilde stood up and leaned over her quarry. "That's bullshit, buddy, and you know it. Tell me what happened, or you're likely to find yourself in very high demand among the state's homosexual prison population. You found out she was cheating? You got angry?" Her voice was growing in volume, while his seemed to be shrinking. "Well?"

The man cowered pathetically. "Yes," he whispered, "I found out for sure. I got angry. But I drove away. I don't remember what happened then, but I wouldn't hurt Alice!"

"Oh, then someone else just happened to come along at the exact moment of your departure? Someone who did *this* to her?" She produced a few Polaroids one of the cops had snapped during her initial investigation of the crime scene. Aisling's face drained of color; he made a horrified sound, shook his head and started to cry. His shaking right hand, attached to the left with a metal link umbilical, brushed new tears off his cheeks while the chain clinked.

"Yeah, that's right," Hilde pressed. The man's eyes were saucers. "Not a pretty picture, is it? It's kind of like the blood's going to drip right out of this photo, huh?"

The trembling suspect whispered, "Oh, God," and puked all over the table. Then he fainted.

Chapter Three

Hagan Lamont was a very busy man. He often said that the last ten years of his law career had been far more profitable and better for his reputation than the first twenty, thanks to a sharp increase in violent crime. That always got a laugh. Four years ago, he'd defended Left Ridge's most notorious murder suspect, Donald Simmons, a cold eighteen-year-old, who had paid two of his friends to kill his mother. Lamont had won the case, against all odds, and soon after his delivery into fame, he'd had to hire a secretary because the phone would not fall silent.

Before long, Lamont had extended an invitation to a partner, then another. If there was such a thing as a "high-powered" attorney in a smaller community like Left Ridge, Hagan Lamont was it. The firm became Lamont, Thompson & Martin, and even the gold watches they all wore like secret decoder rings suggested high-powered tastes.

Hagan Lamont now wished he hadn't wolfed that high-powered double onion jalapeno cheesy chilidog on the way to his meeting with Chief of Police Sarah Janis. Not only did his heart burn like a bright and shining star, but also he had serious doubts about the solidity of his bowels. Tiny, pungent burps were embarrassing enough; now here he was, gazing at crime scene photographs that would turn the stomach of the hungriest man on planet Earth. Stuffing them hastily into his triple gusset Jack Georges satchel, he met Janis' eye and inquired, "So, what have you got?"

"I'm surprised to see you here," Janis said as she scanned her desk. Her office was a complete disaster, right down to the socks sticking out of the file cabinet. Lamont knew for a fact that there were at least three uneaten lunches in one of the desk drawers, and that they had been there since the previous winter. Despite the overall effect, it was true to Sarah's charming form; all of her energy went into other, more vital concerns. "Seems a bit low brow for the almighty Hagan Lamont and his gold watch."

Sarah still stung from their failed relationship. After he'd made it big, they'd drifted apart a little each day, until there was an entire ocean between them. Neither of them had had the strength to paddle. "Judge Dempster ordered me to perform community service to atone for my contempt charge," he replied. "He knew it would sink in more than paying a stupid fine."

"Sure, Hagan. And you have no interest at all in the publicity this case is generating." She knew him well, even two years after their breakup. Headlines drew him like a buzzard to carrion.

"Just lucky, I guess," he said.

Janis produced a clipboard somehow and started to read from it, even though Lamont knew she had already memorized every detail of the arrest. "We have your client's fingerprints, hair, and semen at the scene, we have witnesses who say they heard the couple fighting shortly before the murder. There was a message on the machine from one of the victim's boyfriends. Get this. She was beaten to a pulp with the telephone, then strangled with the cord."

Lamont snorted, though he knew that his well-practiced bluster was wasted on Sarah. "Circumstantial at best! I didn't hear the word 'confession' come out of that pretty and talented mouth," he said. "Just because my client went to see his estranged wife doesn't mean he is the one who killed her. I understand she was quite a busy little bunny."

"Yeah, and that'll speak to motive, you pompous ass. You didn't hear the word 'alibi,' either," Janis retorted. "Your client says he can't remember anything that happened after he left his wife at her sister's." There was a knock at the door; a blonde head poked in. "Yes, Hilde?"

Lamont produced his most winning smile for Hilde Casey; they knew each other and had often found themselves working the same case. She was remarkable and beautiful, Amazon-tall, forty degrees cooler than a cucumber, and renowned for her disdain of men. Not that she liked women any better. She rarely applied makeup and wore her silver-blonde hair in a short, simple style. Hagan knew he had an innocent crush on the detective; hell, who didn't?

"Excuse me, Chief," Casey was saying, "but he's ready for his lawyer."

The interrogation room was painted a demoralizing olive green, and though it was unlikely the cops were clever enough to manipulate the reek in the air, Lamont wouldn't put it past them. Stale sweat and coffee clashed admirably with new carpet smell.

Riley Aisling was slumped in his chair, staring into the wall-sized two-way mirror with haunted eyes. His hands were cuffed, resting on the table in front of him, smudged with black from the fingerprinting. There was also a smudge under his left eye; it was a stark flag on Riley's pale cheek. He didn't seem to notice his lawyer's approach.

"Hi, Riley," Lamont said, sliding into the chair opposite his client, "I'm Hagan Lamont, your friendly neighborhood court-appointed attorney." There was no reply. The guy looked pretty spaced out. Lamont let the silence reign for a few minutes, and then tried again. "Look, Riley, I just want to hear your side of the story, okay? We'll go from there, but you need to trust me. Just tell the truth."

Riley blinked for the first time and shook limp hair out of his eyes. "I..."

"Yes? Go ahead."
"I... don't know the truth."
"What do you mean? Tell me what you remember."
Riley Aisling took a deep, shuddering breath.

The greedy, perilous night devoured the helpless headlight beams; they illuminated only the whirling snowflakes in their bizarre dance around the truck. He couldn't even see the tiny lights of Colevale, and endured a brief yet intense flare of paranoia over whether they were actually there. *Of course they're there.*

Alice's move to her sister's house was a deliberate attempt to be inconvenient; she refused to return to Left Ridge until Riley "treated her right" and learned to be "less suspicious," and certainly not until he "stopped all the insane accusations."

The problem was, Riley reflected, experimenting with the high beams, despite his wary nature, the accusations weren't all that insane. Suspicion had sprouted about a year ago, when Alice's libido hadn't seemed to recognize him. Accusations based on sprouts *were* insane, and Riley knew it—which is why he had waited for more of the weed to grow before confronting Alice. If he were mistaken, a hasty allegation would choke his marriage; he had to give his wife the benefit of the doubt.

It was difficult to ignore hurried, whispered phone calls that ended suddenly upon his arrival in a room. It was exceptionally difficult to ignore Alice's trendy new haircut, her expensive perfume, and her weekly manicures, when none of these self-improvements seemed to be for his benefit!

Finally, he had made a tiny comment—not even a mere ghost of a suggestion—and Alice had exploded, packed up her new wardrobe, and moved out. She "just couldn't live with him when he was like this."

Like this? Like what? Like faithful and committed?

The first night was the worst. Uncertainty, solitude, and apprehension made damnable companions.

Colevale had crept up, unnoticed, and enclosed the truck in muffled, frosty light. Riley repeated the catalyst to himself for the hundredth time as he slowed, gauging the words for any sign of indictment: "Working late again tonight, Hon?" Just as before, the words sounded innocent enough. He was convinced that Alice's guilty conscience had prompted her overreaction.

Riley signaled right, made the turn, and tried not to think about Alice in bed with another man, though the thought was an oily, omnipresent shadow lurking in the back of his mind: His wife's supple lips on another man's flesh—her voice, rising in passion, calling a name that wasn't his. These were the darkest thoughts.

The bright, smiling house welcomed through the raw, murky air. It still twinkled with red and gold Christmas lights; it was just like Junie to procrastinate well into January! Of course his sister-in-law always insisted she was simply partial to lights. She would grin from ear to ear when she learned what effect they had on him as he pressed the Suburban through the crunchy snow in front of the house—his own smile was something to be rediscovered, if only for a moment.

Alice was waiting to unlock the door for him.

It was the most passionate night they had ever shared. She whispered of the children they would have, of her love for him; she promised him her soul, forever and ever. Could she promise her soul to two men? Stifling his suspicion, Riley fell in love all over again, and could not look into the eyes of his wife without believing every caress and every murmured oath. "We are for each other," she breathed as she kissed him, and the breath arose like a song from the sweetest corner of her heart.

They slept soundly, tenderly, warmly, in each other's arms.

The telephone was ringing. It was so early, and so chilly! "Let the machine get it," Alice said sleepily.

Riley smiled and snuggled back down as the machine picked up. It was four o'clock in the morning. There was a pause as the caller's throat was cleared. Alice paled and sat up, and in that single instant, Riley *knew.* He knew! His children would never be conceived. Her soul was an article of trade. He reached his hand out to catch her wrist and, silencing her with a scowl, listened. He waited for the world to detonate, and the Anger squirmed for release.

A man was speaking.

A man wanted to talk to Alice.

A man had gotten her sister's number from a friend. "Baby, I miss you. If you're there, pick up. Please, Alice. I can't wait forever. You promised."

It was like a flash! The Anger seemed to have a grip on his ribcage and was rattling it like the bars of a jail cell! Riley cast off the covers and hurried out of the bed, his face aflame and his feet icy. He clicked on the lamp on the nightstand. Tears were gathering in spicy masses behind his eyes, but he could not allow her to see his humiliation! He had to get dressed! He had to get out of this house!

And the man on the machine yammered on!

"So, yeah, I'll pick you up after work, gorgeous. Can't wait. Later."

Alice flew out of bed, not even bothering to throw on her robe as she approached. Or was her body a bargaining chip, mere apparatus? "Don't," Riley warned. She stopped. "You liar. You *liar.*" Her face looked crumpled, but he didn't care. She deserved it. "I'm leaving."

"No, Riley! I'm sorry! It's not what you think. I *told* him not to phone me anymore!" Her excuses were hollow and brittle, they were empty eggshells, and hadn't they always been?

He couldn't stop his head; it wagged back and forth, left to right. His hands flew around his body like errant hawks. A burning, churning wound had ripped open in the pit of his stomach. "Don't *talk! Shut up!* You're lying *again,* is that all you know how to do? You just spent the whole night making love to me! You actually convinced me that I was imagining your affairs!"

His voice rose and rose until he was shouting, yelling, with all his might and his fear and his anger and she looked scared and he was glad. The Anger seized on the hundreds of agonized nights in a bitter marriage bed; a twisted, twelve-month nightmare of turmoil and doubt; the constant guilt he endured for his mistrust—and Alice denying it all along! "This whole night was nothing but a *lie*, and *you're nothing but a whore*," he screamed at her.

She grabbed her robe and pulled it on. It had yellow bunny rabbits embroidered on the pocket. "Well, I'll be damned! You finally grew a backbone," she shot back, her voice rising to match his. "Pathetic. You don't know how to love me, Riley, and you *never did!*" Her face was red and blotchy; she had mascara smudges under her eyes. "I never should have married a loser like you. I'm too good for you. *I never loved you!*" Her face was wet, but her blue eyes blazed.

The Anger strained against the bars, gaining strength with her every word. Riley looked into his wife's eyes and now saw only scorn. Suddenly it occurred to him that *she* had no right to be angry! His heart was a bleeding, shredded mess, and *she* was yelling at *him*?

With a mighty surge, the Anger snapped the bars.

He knew from experience the power a raised fist could hold. He had never wanted anyone to feel as broken and as vulnerable as he had felt under his father's fist.

Until now.

He advanced on Alice, grinning at her as she backed away with a scream. Riley let her tremble for a minute, tremble and squirm. He enjoyed it, too. He let her scream again—it sounded sincere. Then he said: "I thought you knew me, darling. I would never hit a helpless whore."

She sat in stunned silence as he got dressed, pulled his boots on, and fished for his keys. Riley could smell her tangy shock (he had never yelled at his wife before), and he simply pretended she wasn't there, even when she stood up and crossed her arms. Her voice held an all-too-familiar sneer. "So, you're just leaving? How typical. How typical and pathetic."

He hated wearing gloves—they made his fingers clumsy.

Twice he dropped the keys.

"You're angry, right? Good! Good, at least you're feeling *something*, at least you're reacting! But you don't want to hash it out? Fine, Riley, leave. Asshole. Loser."

The icy air invigorated his skin and cleared his eyes. It was like penetrating a spearmint fog. He slammed the door, as hard as he could, behind him. She always hated it when he slammed the door. Any door.

Riley unlocked the truck and brushed the snow off with a gloved hand. Then, after he got in, he slammed that door, too, for good measure. Alice appeared at the living room window; she was crying even as she flipped him off. Riley gave her a cheery wave and pulled away from Junie's house. His outburst had been so uncharacteristic. Now he felt numb and spacey; his body seemed to be steering without the aid of his conscious mind. He deemed it was entirely possible that he was dreaming, and that there was no way he had loved and left his wife in space of six hours.

Where am I going, anyway? The empty highway stretches out before me.

Where am I going?

Riley shifted in his chair and looked away from the mirror at last. His eyes were wet and red. "Did you know there's an owl outside my cell?" he said. "It stares in at me from its tree."

Lamont ceased his furious note taking and sat back in puzzlement. "An owl?"

"It stares in at me from its tree. It watches me."

"It does?"

"Yes."

"How about that. So, what happened after you drove around some, Riley? Your arraignment's very soon, and I need to know what else happened."

Riley dissolved into tears. "I don't remember. What I do remember..."

"Yes? Tell me."

"You'll think I'm crazy."

Lamont leaned forward to rest manicured fingertips on Riley's wrist. "Already do," he said softly. "But I'm here, I'm on your side. I talked to that young lady cop. What happened? Why were you hallucinating? Are you on LSD or something? Tell me."

Riley took another long, shuddering breath and seemed to regain his composure. Then he pulled up his sleeve. "This wasn't here before," he whispered, offering his arm for Lamont's inspection.

There was an unusual wound on his client's upper arm. It looked like a minuscule ice cream scoop had been used to gouge out some flesh. "There's more," Riley said knowingly, as if the mark were the most significant evidence ever discovered. "I'm having dreams. Bad ones."

Hardly surprising, Lamont thought. Riley Aisling, in an ambitious dive off the deep end, had cracked his skull on the concrete bottom; he was as crazed and sincere as they come. "About Alice?"

Riley seemed taken aback. "Alice? No. *Them*."

"Them?"

"Yeah, them. The grey men. Why me? Why *me*?" The tears returned. "Please help. *Please*."

Lamont sat back, resisting an urge to giggle. His client was obviously suffering from Post-Traumatic Stress; he had seen the symptoms a million times. The question had to be, was Riley nuttier than Mr. Peanut at the time of the murder, or was it a recent development?

"I promise you, I *will* help," he said. "But you must trust me, okay? You're in pretty deep, here, Riley, and I'm the one with the shovel. Understand?" A listless nod. "Good. The first step is to try and get the charges reduced so we can get you out on bail. Tomorrow afternoon, we'll try to get you out of here. Early tomorrow morning, we'll get you a shrink, take your deposition, and start to put together a defense."

"Shrink." Unsurprised.

"Well, you want help, Riley. I think you need it, too. A good place to start is with a shrink."

"Yes." His client looked calmer already—the effect of compassion, and, more than that, proposed action, Lamont supposed. "Thank you."

"You're most welcome."

"Can you do something for me?"

"Name it."

"Can you set up a doctor, to give me a physical? I have to know about the parts of myself that I can't see. I'm sore in all kinds of weird places."

Lamont rose. "That's a good idea," he said. If Riley was more worried about soreness in weird places than sitting in jail mourning the loss of his wife for the rest of his natural life, an insanity defense was the way to go. "I'll see you tomorrow. Try to get some sleep."

His client's chuckle was more of a hoarse bark. "Yeah. Right. I'm starting to think I'll never sleep again."

Hagan Lamont went to the parking lot of the police station, sat in his three-day-old Lexus, and wondered what it would be like to be crazy. He supposed that it was probably a lot like sanity, except that no one believed crazy people because no supporting evidence could prove their crazy theories. This was the key to getting Riley to plead not guilty by reason of insanity, and it was the only chance he had of winning the case. The evidence would win him over, and after he spoke to the shrink, Riley might begin to understand his role in the murder, and agree to let Lamont try to win him his freedom. Welcoming Riley back to reality would have to be Lamont's primary objective.

His cellular phone performed a lively jig against his thigh. It was one of his assistants, Kathleen Kennedy. She had seen the new headlines and wanted to know how his first interview had gone. "Fine," he said as he started the Lexus. "Call up Dr. Walker, tell him I want Riley Aisling thoroughly examined. I want his hands checked for bruises or marks from the telephone cord. I want to know if he's had any drugs or alcohol. I want medical evidence that he committed this crime." Faintly, he could hear Kathleen's pen scribbling madly as he spoke.

"Uh-huh," she said.

"Call up Olga Leonard, tell her to get down here tomorrow morning, too. I want to know exactly what the prosecution is going to use against this client, so we have a valid psychological rebuttal. I want to know whether his memory's shot, or if he's just lying. Also, find me any addresses or phone numbers that will allow me to talk with our client's family, friends, co-workers."

"Uh-huh," Kathleen said again. The pen was still moving, but now she was sipping something, too, probably that damn gourmet coffee she was so devoted to.

"Finally, call up Gina Ross at the *Herald* and fill her in. You know the standard release." The standard release had the word *Lamont* in it approximately twenty times. "Got that?"

"No problem. It's already done."

"Thanks. See you later, Kathy." His stomach growled; apparently the chilidog had retreated.

Chapter Four

After an extremely short time, Riley tired of exploring his cell. The white brick walls and beige-tiled floor were nothing special, the chipped paint on the bars was commonplace, and the stainless steel toilet with its thick blue water and tiny matching sink downright tedious. It was just a cell, like his bedroom in the old days. The cot was looking better and better. Riley lay down and tried to relax; he thought only about the white brick wall and the boring toilet. He may have dozed off, because when he opened his eyes again, it was dark.

And he was not alone.

Though the darkness was complete, Riley could feel them—not just one, an army of them—as they fumbled around in the dark, looking down on him. He could sense their eyes—just like with the cop. But the cop hadn't been watching him when that creepy Dad feeling came over him. Maybe he was wrong now. Maybe he was alone in his cell after all. Confused, Riley tried to move and discovered that he couldn't. "Hey," he protested with numb lips. His tongue felt too heavy to lift. "What? You let me go!"

All at once he found himself levitating like a magician's assistant. He recognized the sensation; it set off echoes in his brain. Terrified now, because he somehow in a flooding rush knew what was coming, he tried to call for help, to scream to anyone that could hear, but his tongue lay completely cold and dead in his mouth as he floated silently, helplessly through the open window. He now knew the awful truth beyond any doubt. He had never wanted to admit it, yet he had suspected it since childhood; even Alice had seemed aware. All control over his life could be given or taken from him at any moment, and his wishes were irrelevant. He, Riley Aisling, was of *absolutely no importance.*

Rage and despair formed a froth of agony that somehow burned through the grey men's paralysis like an acid—if only for a moment. He hit the floor, and even as the door to his cell rattled open, Riley felt his paralysis evaporate. Disoriented, he realized that the guard was helping him to his feet. "Are you okay, man? You were having a nightmare."

Riley sat on his cot. The blankets and pillow were soaked with bitter sweat and his nose was bleeding. "I'm... I'm fine. What time is it?"

"It's four-thirty in the P.M. I wanted to let you know that you have a visitor."

A visitor? "Uh, sure, okay." Fresh apprehension percolated in the pit of his stomach.

The guard left the cell and returned with Riley's visitor in tow, unlocking and relocking the door as he went. The visitor was brawny, tall, and wore a blue wool cap down to his eyebrows. He had mittens on his big hands, and, Riley saw, a face full of piercings. He would probably spring a leak when ingesting fluids.

"Mr. Aisling," Brawny said, wrapping mittened hands around the bars without any introduction, "did they take you to Zeti Reticuli? You have to tell me, I'll understand."

"What?" Riley asked cautiously.

"They picked me, you see, to take with them to Zeti Reticuli. They picked me because I'm special. Are you special, too?"

Riley didn't know what to say, so he said nothing.

"Did they take you? Tell me."

"I don't think so."

"Are you sure? Are you absolutely sure?" Brawny made a fist and hit one of the bars with it. *Bonnggg.*

"Pretty sure."

Brawny withdrew the mittens and started wringing them anxiously. The voice flitted, lost, from Riley's ear to the guard's and around the walls. "He's lying. I know he is. Or, he doesn't remember."

The guard was looking more than a little impatient as he set a heavy palm on the shoulder of the big man. Fortunately, the guard was no slouch in the size department, himself. "You said you knew the prisoner," he said. "He doesn't seem to know you, so I think you'd better go."

"He does, though!" Brawny broke away from the guard's grasp and pressed up against the bars as though he was trying to squeeze between them. "Riley! I am a representative from the Galactic Brethren. We will protect you, and we support you. We know They are coming, we even know why, where, and when. People who have already made contact with Them are considered brethren, Riley, people like you. Come here, take my hand!"

For a moment, Riley could only sit on his cot and hug his knees, but it seemed in that instant that he was shrinking away from himself. It shamed him that he was colored by the bright alarm and pity of those who wondered to where and when his mind had departed. He rose from the creaky cot and stretched his hand out to the mitten.

"A wonderful time is coming, Riley," Brawny said, squeezing Riley's hand, "and you are very special. Soon, all will be understood."

Riley smiled. This was the moment to accept rather than attack, to give freely the benefit of the doubt that had been denied him. "I don't know what you're talking about," he said, looking up into warm brown eyes, "but I believe you. Thank you for coming to see me."

"Let's go," the guard insisted, taking a firmer grasp on Brawny's shoulder. "Come on, come with me."

The creature at the gates had returned. Fortified by the conversations of the day, it now heaved at the floodgates with more power than before, and Riley wasn't sure he would be able to keep it out this time. The thing terrified him; he knew somehow that it was a bizarre, greedy monstrosity. If it were released, Riley knew it could hurt him terribly. But did he have the strength to keep it confined?

He took deep breaths and thought about his nightmare, and about his late afternoon visitor. Could the grey men haunting him actually be aliens? To his surprise, the notion stuck. He had never believed in UFO reports or that Roswell stuff, always assuming that the people involved in those stories were either lying or crazy. It wasn't so much that he didn't believe in life out there; it was more like he had never seriously considered the possibility until now. There was enough to worry about on *this* planet, with *this* species, and within *this* life.

The floodgates were inching open; Riley was too deep in thought to notice.

Alice. Who had killed her? Riley suspected one of her lovers. What if he had stayed to talk to her? What if he hadn't bolted out of the house at that moment? What if the phone hadn't rung?

His own imagination haunted him with supposition: Alice, torn and trampled and desperate, clawing for a gulp of air and life as the telephone cord bites into her supple throat. Her eyes, an angry, bloody color, bulge in their sockets; her face is a dark bruise and her body performs an awful frantic dance. Alice's killer is faceless yet masculine, standing just behind her. He heaves at the twisted cord in one hand and reaches around to squeeze her breast with the other as she suffers defeat. He whispers something in her ear, but Riley doesn't want to hear! *I can't hear her breathing...* He doesn't want to think about this any more! *Her tongue is a black balloon...*

The creature at the gates wasn't as fearsome now; in fact it seemed a welcome alternative to *this* torment. Hoping for relief at its interference, Riley approached the floodgates and stood before them a moment, head bowed, listening for the giant thing. *I can't hear her breathing...* With a shock, Riley realized it was *now*, the time was *now*, and no more excuses or he would really screw up royally, maybe the creature would retreat forever to leave him with his own appallingly vivid imagination. With a slight glance around, he took hold of the iron rings and pulled at them.

Chapter Five

Doctor Jason Walker arrived at six o'clock a.m. to inspect Riley's body, as requested. Regular consults for Lamont, Thompson & Martin tore him away from his beloved O.R., but he was paid very well for his valuable time, even when the consult hardly warranted the attention of a brilliant surgeon. Because he slummed now and then, and kept his mouth shut, his yearly income was around a hundred and seventy-five thousand dollars a year, after taxes. At only twenty-seven, single, blond, and fit, his money made him insufferable, and he knew it. Actually, he delighted in it.

The patient regarding him at the moment was wearing a ten-dollar Wal-Mart special. Doctor Walker rolled his eyes and went to wash his hands in the small stainless steel sink. He let cold water run over them for a minute or two before he pulled gloves over them. "Any pain or soreness?" he asked with a yawn, as the patient got undressed.

"Yes. I'm sore in my genitals and... you know, further down south. Also, something's giving me nosebleeds. But first, can you check my skin for any more of these?"

Doctor Walker could not conceal a frown at the sight of the small scoop wound. "What's that?"

"I'm not sure. I think they took some samples."

Though the doctor didn't normally encourage conversation from patients, especially murder suspects, in this instance he simply could not resist. "They?"

"Yeah, doc. They." The man was an inarticulate bore. No surprise there.

Walker sent his icy fingertips across the sweaty, twitching flesh; they pressed expertly and firmly as they traveled. There *were* more of those marks on the back and buttocks, as well as some older scars with the same shape. There were also numerous old scars with different shapes. "Are you having any internal pain?"

"I'm kind of sore all over. It hurts when I breathe in and when I go to the bathroom," the suspect replied, wincing.

This was more interesting than he had expected. Walker favored the patient with a thin smile. "Would you consent to a body scan? I'd like to see if you have any internal injuries."

"Okay. Whatever. Please, can you check my nose?"

"Very well." Walker rummaged in his medical bag for his otoscope. "Tilt your head back." The patient complied and the instrument slid up his nose.

"There is something very familiar about this sensation," the man said, not moving his head. "It makes me queasy."

Like I care? Annoyed, Walker snapped, "Quiet." There was nothing in the left nasal cavity; he slid the instrument into the right. Something glinted, like a wink in guttering candlelight. "What the hell is that?"

"Wha?"

"Ssh. There's... something... shiny..." The doctor extended a steady hand toward his instrument tray and found the extractor without even casting a glance. "I may need to call some colleagues," he said, more to himself than to his patient. He much preferred talking to himself.

The shrink arrived at nine o'clock a.m. to inspect Riley's mind, as requested. They rendezvoused, with two or three pairs of eyes watchful always, in the gloomy interrogation room, which apparently didn't see much action. The doctor's snowy hair was drawn up into a loose bun; gold-rimmed spectacles hung around her neck. She had a plump frame and wore an old-fashioned navy dress with tiny white polka dots and sensible shoes. Her hazel eyes were amiable; she wore no makeup. "Do you understand your situation?"

"Of course I do. I'm stuck here until the trial, because everyone thinks I'm lying, or dangerous, or crazy."

"I'm sorry about that, Riley. I know Hagan tried very hard to get you out on bond. It happens that way sometimes. Anyway, you know why you're here? In jail?"

"Yes. I'm going on trial for murdering my wife, even though I have an alibi."

"Do you?"

"Yes. I remembered last night. I was abducted…by alien life forms. While I was a prisoner on their ship having scoops of flesh removed from eight different parts of my body and multiple devices stuck down my throat, up my ass, in my nose and penis, someone murdered my wife."

"You sound angry. Why do you think aliens played a part in this?"

"Why do I think they did? Or why did they?"

"Both."

"Well, I didn't want to believe it, but the physical evidence abounds."

"Such as?"

"How about the thing the doctor took out of my nose? How about the marks on my body? Then, there's the flashbacks, the dreams, the paranoia. Not about killing Alice, but about being abducted. I'm starting to think they've been visiting me for a long time, maybe even my whole life. I can't begin to guess at their purpose, but I wish they hadn't picked me. I wish they hadn't picked me!"

"So," the shrink said, leaning back in her chair and pressing her fingertips together, "you want to use this alien alibi for your defense?"

"It's what happened."

"And do you expect a jury to believe you?"

"It's what happened."

The shrink flipped to the next page in her little yellow notebook. "What else would you like to talk about today?"

"Gee, let me guess. You want to talk about my wife. Or, better yet, my parents."

The shrink smiled. It was a warm and sunny beam, and Riley felt a twinge of guilt at his sarcasm. "Are those things you want to talk about?" she asked in a voice to match her smile.

It was long ago. Daddy was angry. As usual, Riley wasn't sure why Daddy was angry, but he knew it had to be his fault. It seemed like Daddy was mad most of the time.

One time, he had been in his room playing with his trains, and Daddy had busted in, and stepped all over his trains on purpose and broke them. The sounds of his beloved trains cracking under Daddy's big boots filled the room, and all Riley could do was sit and stare as his only friends were destroyed. That's the first time Mommy whispered under her breath, "It's the booze, sweetie," but he didn't know what that meant. His heart hurt to look at his trains, trampled and ruined, but his heart hurt even more to look at his sick, angry Daddy, and at his Mommy, who was looking trampled and ruined herself.

That was a while ago, maybe a couple of years ago or something, when he was five. He was a big boy now, he was seven, he had new friends, and he still didn't know why Daddy got so angry, or why he was so mean sometimes. Riley and his Mommy tried hard to be good and stay out of Daddy's way, but sometimes they *screwed up royally*. That's what Daddy said a lot when he was mad: "Oh this time you *screwed up royally*."

That's what he was saying right now, and he was saying it to Riley.

Even though he had no idea of how he had *screwed up royally*, Riley told his Daddy he was sorry. If he said anything other than "I'm sorry, Daddy," he would be in *really* big trouble, so he never did.

"You bet you're sorry," Daddy replied, "and you're going to be sorrier."

Riley never found out how he had *screwed up royally.* It didn't really matter anyway.

Doctor Olga Leonard nodded her snow-capped thoughtfully. The story was a familiar one to her. "Do you still believe you're to blame for your father's temper? His violence?"

The patient closed his eyes a moment. "No," he said. "And yes. I'm sorry."

"It's perfectly all right, Riley," she said kindly, and offered him an oatmeal cookie out of a paper bag she'd brought. She made excellent oatmeal cookies and never skimped on the raisins. "You just gave me a very normal, very human answer to my question. You needn't apologize." The doctor wrote two words in her notebook here as Riley ate his cookie: *Vicious cycle.*

She had been around long enough to recognize a second or even third-generation abuse victim. Doctor Leonard thought it very likely that Riley's father had started out his life as a victim himself. As he grew, the victim became the victimizer out of a sheer panic for control over his life; he also sought escape through alcohol and drugs. The more out of control his life got, the more violent and paranoid he became.

"Did you like living with your foster parents, Riley?"

"I love Vi and Harry very much."

It was a real shame. The sensitive young man before her was undoubtedly on the same road as his father, and the road led straight to the chair.

Here's where it got tricky, though, and she would need more time to ascertain whether the suspect was responsible for his actions.

As if on cue, Riley asked a suitably bizarre question: "Are we going to talk about the aliens?"

Once more, she flipped to a new page in her notebook. "We're going to talk about whatever you want." She leaned forward conspiratorially; Riley accepted her into his space. *He's starting to trust me.* Over the years, Doctor Leonard had perfected ways to earn a patient's trust, like the cookies.

The more a patient trusted her, the more she could help. She sometimes pretended to share convictions simply to that end. "Personally, I would love to hear about these fascinating visitors."

It was long ago, lying painfully on his bed, that Riley first imagined his daddy was a hideous monster. Only monsters chased you down and hurt you for no reason, wasn't that so? Only monsters hid under your bed or in your closet just to watch you and scare you, wasn't that so? Daddy was scary, all right, but most terrifying of all, if he wasn't a monster, that meant all of Riley's pain was his own fault, and since he always tried to be a good boy, there must be something very wrong with him. Probably he was half monster himself. Wasn't that so?

He hated himself for it, but every night his heart would swell in terror at the thought of Daddy hiding in the closet, whether he was in there or not. It wasn't safe to ever believe that he was by himself, but usually he could relax enough to fall asleep. Inevitably, moments before sleep came, the same fantasy would surface: Escape from this house, from his daddy-monster. He and Mommy could just bust out and escape. Of course the fantasy never solidified; he was too weak and scared, and Mommy was too broken to ever escape from Daddy.

Tonight, as Riley laid hurting and wondering upon his Ghostbusters sheets with the guts and bones of his slaughtered trains buried in a dusty box under his bed, the big light started to shine through his window. He could hear Daddy snoring in the room across the hall; he could hear his alarm clock ticking. The big light didn't make a sound.

It had come before, Riley remembered suddenly, maybe a couple of times, a long time ago, and it had caressed his mind with whispery fingers. *Do not fear us*, the whisper told him, and, at only three, he had accepted without question. Now the light was back, bluish and blinding, but there was no voice in his mind this time, only a rising panic that was quelled in an instant with a single thought: Anywhere, anything, is better than this cell with the daddy-monster in the closet. When the light started to pull him toward the window, he did not resist, not that he could have.

The next morning made the experience dreamlike, and Riley found himself wondering if it had happened at all. He couldn't remember what had happened after he'd left his room. Could it be he never had? But Daddy knew, and he was angry; his own kid had snuck out in the middle of the night! His own kid! Riley didn't argue—he didn't know how. "I'm sorry, Daddy," was all he could say, as always, and stop thinking about the warming hope budding in his heart and mind.

Escape was possible.

Chapter Six

Hagan Lamont gathered his staff and met the two doctors at his usual table at a very chic restaurant; it was his habit to hold meetings at *Daven's* so the press could circle like sharks, but not strike. It was poor etiquette to interrupt a luncheon, and even if the scent of blood drew more than a few sharks, they maintained safe distances. Kathleen had today's paper under her arm; Victor Martin had the case file in tow. Lamont ordered for them all—Smoked Duckling and Forest Mushroom Tostada; a bit heavy for lunch, true, but he felt he owed his stomach an apology for the chilidog. The waiter had a huge ingratiating grin on his face and actually bowed as he departed for the kitchen.

While they waited, they sipped an excellent Zinfandel.

Kathleen produced the paper, smoothed it lovingly, and spread the front page on the table. "Did Aisling mention anything about an afternoon visitor he had yesterday to either of you?" she asked the doctors. "Because whoever it was went straight to the press with this crazy alien story."

"Alien story?" Lamont was intrigued. Riley's delusions had progressed—first grey men, now aliens. "Let me see that."

The headline was *UFO Group Vouches for Murder Suspect*. "Hmm, Galactic Brethren, eh? A group of wackos vouching for another—that'll hold a lot of water." He paused. "Hey! They only mention us twice."

"Well, this story is running all over the country. I wouldn't be surprised if it made its way into the international press. This is bigger than the Simmons case." Kathleen was getting excited. Zinfandel always went straight to her head.

"Don't get too worked up yet," Victor Martin interjected. "We still have to win."

"It'll never get to court," Lamont said. "The guy's totally nuts. Right, doc?"

They had joked for years that Olga Leonard looked completely out of her element in *Daven's*. She was definitely the country bed-and-breakfast type, with her plump physique and white hair drawn up into its loose bun.

"In my professional opinion, the defendant is suffering from Post Traumatic Stress disorder, the aftermath of a breakdown. He is experiencing hallucination and delusion so practiced from an abused childhood that they appear seamless to him. Unfortunately, he expects a jury to accept his delusions as the truth." Resisting the wine, she sipped her water.

"Just like I said. The guy's totally nuts."

"However," Dr. Leonard continued, as though Lamont had not spoken, "his mental capacity at this moment has little bearing on his case. What's important is that the breakdown came either immediately before or during the murder. During that time, Mr. Aisling's brain took over, and then created an alibi to suppress his own guilt regarding the crime."

Lamont inspected the silverware, idly, for crusties or lipstick. "You're saying that Riley is, at this moment, clinically insane? Damn! I was planning to hook him up to a polygraph. There wouldn't be much point in that."

"Exactly. He can only believe what his own brain is telling him, you know. And his brain is telling him that he did not commit this crime because aliens had him on their ship."

Victor looked doubtful. "Why didn't his brain concoct a story that would actually get him off the hook? Why this crazy alibi?"

Dr. Walker, taking silent advantage of the complimentary breadsticks, washed his latest mouthful down with some Zinfandel. "If I may, Doctor? Perhaps the suspect has adopted this alibi as a means of overcoming an overwhelming remorse for killing his wife. The alibi is a way to atone without admitting his guilt. He's turned himself into a victim, rather than a victimizer. I haven't found any physical evidence of the murder, yet, but I did find some other suspicious evidence."

The young doctor raised both his hands and made invisible apostrophes with his fingers around "evidence." Kathleen giggled shamelessly as he continued, "I did some research and found that this "evidence" would be generally accepted by your common everyday UFO freak, or even a genuine ufologist, if you believe there's difference between the two. In fact, it's like it came off a list."

He produced a baggie from a roomy pocket and passed it to Lamont. "I really think this evidence was planted by the patient to support his fantasy. I'm having it analyzed by a specialist."

Lamont inspected the contents of the baggie. "What is this thing? It's heavy! A little metal barbell…" The shape was irregular; the silver-grey metal gleamed dully beneath the mood lighting of the restaurant.

"I found it inside Aisling's nasal cavity. Once we prove its Earthly origins, I think we can convince him he put it there himself. Hopefully, he'll be willing to play ball and let you try the insanity defense."

"Very good," Dr. Leonard agreed. "We are amassing the tools to bring Mr. Aisling down to Earth." She patted at her hair in grandmotherly satisfaction. "By shattering his protective delusion, we could see one of two effects. One, he might begin to understand his crime and participate in his own defense. Two, his mind could shatter when he realizes that, based on his actions, he's no better than his father."

"Father?" Lamont asked.

"Yes, you must remember the case. Years ago—I don't recall how many now—his father brutally murdered the mother, and got the death penalty."

"Riley's the kid? No shit! Didn't he see the whole thing?"

"Yes."

"Well, that's not our problem," Lamont said. "That's the state's problem. Our only concern is eliminating or minimizing the time Riley serves for this crime, got it? The best way to do that is to prove he was not responsible for his actions the night of the murder, that the message on the machine actually drove him into a homicidal rage. If we can do that, the prosecution just may offer us a deal."

"Shouldn't be too hard," Kathleen mused as lunch arrived, hot and fragrant. Lamont and his team always got their order in record time. "The detective in charge of the case is trying to find the guy on that machine. She can help the jury understand why his message made Riley's brain crack."

"Excellent. Let's eat, people. We have work to do."

As soon as Lamont and his entourage left, the waiter stuffed the sizeable tip into his right pocket and waved at a diner sitting across the restaurant. After returning the wave, the man pushed his chair back and crossed the room. The two did a quick scan, and determining that the coast was clear, stooped to peer under the table.

"Nice going, man," said the patron.

There was a slight ripping sound—tape peeling—before the waiter produced a micro cassette recorder. Gleefully, the man rewound the tape and played a snippet of conversation, listening with a smile to the lawyers' banter. Then, he took a cell phone from his pocket and hit the redial button.

"Hey, it's Mike. You're not gonna believe what I just got on tape!"

The waiter cleared his throat, his hand out. Mike nodded and slapped a hundred into his sweaty palm.

"Thanks for your help, man. As usual, very discreet."

Back into the cell phone:

"I'm on my way right now. What I wouldn't give to see those lawyers open tomorrow's paper!"

Lunch was macaroni and cheese with gritty coleslaw and canned fruit cocktail. As he ate, Riley thought about the future. He tried to imagine confronting his first wrinkles, tried to imagine plucking his first grey hair, and wondered if he would age alone in front of a prison mirror.

He thought of all the common symptoms of old age—aches and pains, little mental failings—and imagined welcoming them alone, with no grandchildren to kiss his cheek. He remembered what his father had looked like behind bars, and knew that he was looking at himself.

If he were ever released, how would he know what to do? How could he make it alone? Riley blocked the panic rising at the thought of himself, as an old man, talking to the owl outside, and reflecting on all his past years in his cell, his whole life, practically. The only time he'd been truly free was when he'd been with Alice. He was beginning to think that death might be his only escape.

Riley closed his eyes and imagined he was sitting in the Chair. He put his hands on the armrests and lay back, listening to the bustle around him. There were silent people seated in an adjoining chamber; silent people had come to watch him die. They'd come to watch him fry. He saw faces he knew—his inlaws, his foster parents, Junie. How could she have that look on her face? It was a look of pleasant anticipation.

The bustle around him quieted; one voice sailed out alone. It was the Lord's Prayer. Riley felt a warm wetness on the top of his newly-shaved head, and then...

The Helmet. The Helmet was buckled over his head. As it was brought down over his eyes, Riley saw Junie wave goodbye. She had a smile on her face.

There was a moment of perfect silence, in which Riley could hear his horrified heart pounding hard in his chest; the air came in and out of his lungs in short, panicky bursts. Then a voice said, "May God have mercy on your soul," and there was a sound like a huge breaker being thrown.

Riley felt nothing, but he could smell himself cooking like a Sunday roast. He knew his brain was about to liquefy, he knew his heart was held, motionless, in the streams of electricity. Soon it would all be over.

No one would mourn.

No one would miss him.

There would be no funeral.

But he would be free.

"Riley?" A voice brought him out of his morbid fantasy, brought him back to his dented cell with its tiny sink. The voice was brimming with tenderness; it was a voice he knew and loved and missed. Vi and Harry were standing outside his cell.

"Hello, boy," Harry said, and put his arm around his wife. "We came as soon as we could. It's good to see you."

Chapter Seven

The morning of the arraignment was cold and crisp, but warm for January. Hagan Lamont parked his Lexus in front of the courthouse and waited for the cops to bring his client. A throng of media had already gathered on the courtroom steps; Lamont tilted his rearview mirror to check between his teeth and try on a few smiles. He had an image to uphold after all, and that image was strong, confident, and impeccable, despite his clientele.

Opening the morning paper had been a shock, especially since the news hit him at exactly 6 a.m., before he'd had his first cup of coffee.

The headline read "Wife-killer Spaced Out" and provided more information than he had planned to impart to the press. Hoping the damage was only local, he threw a coat over his pajamas and dashed to the local convenience store to check the rest of the state's headlines. "Out-Of-This-World Alibi!" cried one; "Aisling's Alien Alibi!" heralded another. There was even one that had already decided, "Lamont's Impossible Dream." Who had been the fly on the wall? It didn't much matter; it was too late to swat—besides, it was gratifying to see one's own name in a headline at last.

Lamont pulled a comb out of his glove compartment and gave his salt-and-pepper hair a smoothing as a patrol car pulled up beside him. Riley looked white, weary, and petrified as Lamont got out of his car and approached. He also seemed mesmerized by the large crowd of media.

"Don't worry about the sharks," Lamont said into his ear as they started up the steps. "They have a taste of your blood now; they're excited and greedy. Just keep walking and don't speak."

The media circled, thoughtfully. They seemed to be gauging the footsteps of their prey, waiting for a sublime moment to strike. When they crashed in on all sides to shout their questions and snap their teeth at one another, it was as Lamont and his client mounted the landing before the doors. The voices collided and exploded all around, and suddenly a wall of bodies erased the path to the doors.

"Clear the way, please!" called out the cop ahead of them. "Come on, move it!" Access to the doors was slowly returned, and, breathless, Lamont and his client were ushered inside.

Even through the glass, Riley could hear the voices of the sharks.

The arraignment went pretty much as Hagan Lamont expected. The charge the prosecution had settled on, predictably: Murder in the First Degree. Riley still refused to plead not guilty by reason of insanity. Instead, he insisted that he was innocent, that he had an alibi, and that the cops should be looking for the real killer. Unimpressed, the judge denied bail. Riley was very lucky to live in a small community. In a large city, Lamont knew his client would rot in jail for months before his case ever went to trial.

Riley's trial date was set to begin in two weeks, with hanging Judge Dwight Dempster presiding. Two weeks, Lamont thought, to change his client's mind. The insanity defense would almost guarantee an acquittal; a jury could be easily convinced that Riley was not in his right mind at the time of the killing, that the message left by Alice's lover had sent him over the edge. He had two weeks to prove to his client that his alibi was a fabrication of his own brain.

First things first, however, and the first thing was a meeting with the bitchy assistant D.A. and chief prosecutor in this case, Andreana Keene for a little plea-bargaining. Her office was gorgeous and bright, feminine yet sturdy. Men seemed absurdly out-of-place. It seemed very deliberate and sneaky to Lamont.

"What are you offering?" he asked, in his most bored voice.

"Aggravated manslaughter, fifteen to twenty-five," she said in an equally bored voice.

Lamont shook his head calmly. "Please!" he said. "If my client committed this crime, which is certainly open to conjecture, he did it in the heat of passion, and may well have been insane at the time of the murder. Fifteen to twenty-five? No can do."

"I wouldn't be so hasty if I were you," Keene said. "I've uncovered evidence that your client knew all along that his wife was cheating. If that were the case, the message on that machine would not have been so great a shock, would it? Makes you question the whole 'pushed over the edge' motive, doesn't it?"

Lawyers had to play by the rules; as a result, they were extraordinary bluffers, and in time, they learned to read their opponents well. Lamont sincerely hoped he was seeing Keene's poker face at this moment, but he knew that smirk; it invariably made him nervous. Keene continued, "If we go to trial, and that jury comes back with a guilty verdict on the murder one charge, your client will get a maximum sentence. He could even get the death penalty."

"Thanks, I was wondering how that worked. I'm going to have to get back to you after I consult with my client."

"Fine. You do that." Her eyes followed him as he moved into the hallway.

Hagan Lamont loved his cell phone. It saved him so much legwork that he wished he could make it a partner in the firm. He dialed Left Ridge Detention Center, a number that he knew by heart, and asked to speak to his client. It was a short wait, then Riley was on the other end: "Hello?"

"Hi, Riley, it's me. How you holding up?"

"Just great." Sarcasm! That was new.

"The D.A. offered a deal, it'll carry a minimum fifteen year penalty, but chances are, you'll serve more like five. You would plead guilty to aggravated manslaughter. I think you should consider it. The alternative could be…"

"No!" his client cried. "You lawyers aren't going to pull me back and forth like a scrap of meat between hyenas!" Riley was angry, but at the same time, Lamont heard a tightness in his client's throat that could only be tears. "Is this how you support me, believe in me, help me? I'm innocent, damn it! I will not plea-bargain. Do you hear me? I did not kill my wife. What the hell kind of a defense lawyer are you?"

The silence that followed was potent enough to wilt even Lamont's ego. "Okay, Riley. You're the boss."

He hung up and poked his head back into the bright, sturdy office. "My client says no deal. We'll see you in court," he said to Keene.

Chapter Eight

The small white stucco house with the blue trim had a tall pine tree in the front yard and tiger lilies flourishing in its perimeter flowerbeds. There were two doors, one at the very front of the house, and one nearer the left side; he had already received instructions to enter through the side door. *We don't really use the door in the front room.* As Lamont put his car into park and headed up the walk, the moss-green kitchen curtain flickered aside for a moment, revealing an elderly woman with a welcoming smile.

Her grin was daylight itself compared to the dark lack of response he'd gotten from Riley's in-laws, who would not even deign to speak with him. He'd tried phoning, he'd tried e-mailing, and he'd attempted a few personal visits. Finally, there was no option but to apply for a subpoena.

In the meantime, Riley's foster parents had no objection to an interview—in fact, they were eager to help. As he approached the side door and knocked, Lamont could see a tiny tool shed and a modest garage in the back yard. There was also what appeared to be some kind of run-down guesthouse opposite the tool shed, on the other side of the yard. It was white, but the windows were dirty brown. Lamont was curious, but a voice from inside the house beckoned him; he entered the small foyer and then took a right to mount the few steps into the kitchen.

Cigarette smoke associated freely with oxygen in this house, often even gaining the upper hand. A portable transistor radio was tuned to the local country music station; Hank Williams was wondering what good lookin' could possibly have cookin'. Lamont cast a glance around the cozy kitchen: Fridge on his direct right, sink a little ways up on the right, stove straight ahead, table on the left. The kitchen windows with their moss-green curtains were over the sink.

The smiling elderly woman stood at the sink; at the table sat a bald older man, smoking, with his back to Lamont. The table was cluttered with newspapers, shopping lists, Kleenex, ashtrays, cookies, rolling papers, and tobacco. On the wall over the table were numerous pictures of golden-haired children, probably the grandkids.

"Come in, come in," said the woman at the sink. "I'm Vi. This is Harry." She ushered Lamont to the table and pulled up a chair opposite her husband. "How about a cup of tea or coffee? Or maybe you're hungry? Would you like a sandwich or something?"

Lamont chuckled. Though his mother had never touched the dial on her own stove, he knew from three decades of legwork that resistance to grandmotherly types was futile. "A cup of tea would be nice," he said. Harry nodded approvingly; he had a mug of tea to his own lips.

"Saw you looking at the pictures," Vi said chattily as she poured Lamont's tea. "Those are the grandkids."

"That's what I thought," Lamont said. "They're cute. Are they your biological grandchildren?"

"Oh, yes. We had four strong boys all grown up before Riley came."

Four boys? This woman was tougher than she looked, especially now as she set his tea in front of him. Her hands were knotted with what could only be arthritis. "What do you remember about what Riley was like when he first came here?"

Vi pulled a stool out from under the table and sat upon it. "I remember everything," she said. "Riley was almost sixteen, skinny, bruised, with scars all over him and haunted eyes from here to the floor." Harry had started nodding as he smoked and drank his tea. "They sent him to us because we know boys," she added.

No kidding, lady. "What can you tell me about his mental state? Was his behavior odd or disturbing in any way?" The tea was good—really, really strong and twice as sweet.

"I don't know about disturbing, but odd for sure. Jesus, who could blame him? So he acted a little weird once in awhile, so what? At least he was alive, at least he was safe." Harry's nodding had become more vigorous. Vi reached for a cigarette; there were eight or ten scattered around on the table. She lit up, and then said as she exhaled menthol smoke, "He had nightmares, actually night terrors, and I think he sleepwalked because a few times I found his bed empty in the middle of the night and Riley never knew where he'd been."

Lamont sat up straighter at this. What if Riley's memory had betrayed him in the past? If a pattern could be found, it would skyrocket Riley's credibility. "How old was Riley when he moved out?"

"Well, he moved into the guesthouse when he turned twenty-two, so when he left... he was twenty-five. He was very happy here, and we took care of each other, but he fell in love with Alice and moved in with her." Vi's crepe-paper face crinkled even more. "I always thought he loved the idea of Alice more than he loved Alice herself, and that the same was true for her. I never expected their marriage to last."

"The idea of Alice," Lamont repeated thoughtfully, a headline flashing in his brain: *Riley the Downtrodden Weds Upper-Class Princess.* Damn—tough, insightful, and memory brighter than a digital picture, Violet Langhofer was a living example of The Reliable Witness. "You'll testify, I assume?"

Vi crushed out her cigarette in one of the ashtrays and stood, pushing the stool back under the table as she did so. Her eyes were suddenly glittery.

"Of course she will," Harry said. "You just write down what we need to do, and we'll do it."

After playing the answering machine back dozens of times, it was nearly ten o'clock. Hilde Casey had finally discovered a clue.

"So, yeah, I'll pick you up after work, gorgeous. Can't wait. Later."

In between the words *work* and *gorgeous*, there was another voice, only audible when the volume was at full. The voice was a man's, and even though it was tangled in with background hiss and the words *work* and *gorgeous*, it was now plain to Hilde that it formed a word. Just what that word was still wasn't clear.

"Ache?" she mused aloud. "Maybe *hey*." She rewound the tape without sparing it a glance and played it again. The long *A* sound mocked her efforts; there was no way to tell what the voice was saying. Discouraged, Casey sat back and considered her warm, soft bed, a complete opposite environment from her chilly office with its concrete chair. The temptation to go home was powerful, yet she didn't feel all that weary. Perhaps her mind simply wanted a change of scenery.

What would be a change of scenery for Alice Aisling, a woman who thrived on excitement and change? What would be a departure from her nice home, a departure from her nice husband and nice parents and nice job? A change of scenery would be the opposite of nice. A change of scenery would be nasty.

Hilde Casey thought about some of the nasty scenes she had worked as a police sergeant. Alleys, flophouses, drug houses, and bars. Which of these would appeal to a woman like Alice Aisling, who was used to getting what she wanted and lived in the fast lane? *Think, Detective. Think.* Of the drug houses and bars, each were of equal nastiness, but the drug houses were actually quite dangerous, and it was quite impossible to maintain control over any situation—especially for a rich white woman. Hilde doubted that the victim would put herself into such a position.

Her phone rang, suddenly, making her jump. Annoyed with herself, Casey answered with a sharp "Yes?"

"I have those phone records for you, Detective," said the voice on the other end. "Would you like me to fax them to you?" Hilde said she did, then hung up and waited for the transmission.

She wanted to like Riley Aisling for the murder, it would keep this nice and neat, but something just wasn't right. Riley Aisling didn't *feel* like the right guy, and Hilde knew herself well enough to accept this—often a feeling was all she had to go on. Her interrogation of the suspect had been plagued by an unexpected response: *I don't remember.* She trusted her instincts, and either the suspect was telling the truth about not killing Alice Aisling, or he was the Tiger Woods of lying.

Another reason she had problems with men, she supposed, was that Hilde Casey was trained to know when someone was lying to her. She read eye movement and body language the way most people read words—and none of Aisling's behavior flagged her. Besides, it was her job to ferret out any other leads or suspects, on the assumption that the suspect was innocent until found guilty by a jury of his peers.

Something else was bothering her, too. Why did the name Riley Aisling strike her as so familiar? Hilde was certain she knew the name, but not how or why.

The fax rang, connected, and started its electronic chatter. The phone records began to arrive in long, spooling reams of paper; the words and the numbers were tiny and smudged. Hilde dialed Hagan Lamont.

Chapter Nine

Riley didn't sleep much nowadays; it was like being a child again. Sometimes he dozed off, but never for more than a couple of hours, when his eyes would flip open with no permission from the rest of the body or brain. It was around ten thirty or so, and he had just started awake once again, when the guard came to his door and inserted the key. "You have, like, a bunch of mail, man."

"Mail?"

"Yeah, a whole sack. Thought it might help to pass the time, you know?"

The sack was about the size of a kitchen catcher bag, and it was stuffed with envelopes. The guard set the sack on the floor just inside the door, then relocked it and retreated to his desk to watch Star Trek. Riley could hear the theme music faintly as he upended the sack. Envelopes in all shapes, sizes, and colors spilled out all over the floor. Riley could see drawings and writing on the backs of many of them; curious, he selected one because of its friendly pink and opened it.

Mr. Riely,
Your story has captured the attention of the entire country. We think it's despicable that you would tell stories rather than confess to your sin. Don't you know you're going to Hell?

You're a murderer of women. Good luck with your defense, you'll need it!
The Nelsons

The entire country? How had he become a murderer of women, in the plural, overnight? Could it be that the entire country hated him? Riley tore the letter up and chose another, hoping the Nelsons did not represent the majority.

Mr. Aisling,
Do you really expect us to believe aliens abducted you? How did you come up with this stuff? I think you're in big trouble—if I were on the jury, you'd be in the chair already. People like you don't deserve to live.
Shelley

Horrified, Riley tore up this letter, too, and hurled the pieces into the air. They drifted back down like giant arid snowflakes. Though he hated the idea of opening any more "fan mail," a tiny tickle next to his heart convinced Riley that he would not be able to rest until he'd found at least one letter of support. *Nobody believes you... you're a killer... you're a liar... you're insane...* Dismay slowly became exhaustion, and hours later he found himself dozing over a colorful heap of shredded paper.

The house was a prison, for both him and his mommy. Even though it had a garden, and a big sunny kitchen, and comfy old blue furniture in the living room, it was a prison nonetheless; Daddy was the warden. Riley was slowly warming to the idea that someday, he might take his mommy away to be free. He'd gone before, out the window, and nothing really bad had happened. This time he would leave on his own, and he would never come back. Wasn't fifteen years enough time to spend in prison, especially for an innocent pair? Riley spent a lot of time in his room; it was his cell, but at least he didn't have to deal with his father. It was easy to stay out of the way in his cell, even though Daddy had long ago removed the door.

Mommy's cell was just across the hall, across the gold carpet, but it had a door, and Mommy was often behind it. Riley could hear her crying through the door almost every day. That sound, more than any other torment his father inflicted, was the reason Riley wanted to escape. Icy fists of fear squeezed his spine and the base of his skull... what would Daddy do to them if he caught them? And where would they go?

Away, Riley told himself. Away is all that matters.

He awoke with a start, stiff-necked, dry-mouthed, and hands bloody from paper cuts. He was only half way through the pile of mail, yet had encountered only jeers and condemnations and disbelief. Riley doubted that he could open another single letter; they all thought he was a killer, and they all wanted him to die. It was becoming increasingly difficult to continue picking himself up after constant shoves to the cold ground, and worse yet, he was afraid the letters might convince even him. Sadly, he began to stuff the rest of the letters into the bag, when his eye fell upon an envelope of lime green, with two words written on the back in red:

We Believe!

Riley's heart leapt absurdly; what did the opinion of one matter against the tide of thousands?

It did matter, though.

It mattered *a lot*.

Dear Mr. Aisling,

My sister and I are very sorry for your predicament. It's quite unfortunate that our cosmic friends chose that precise moment to "borrow" you; we hope the jury believes your alibi. Here is a list of your supporters in our area: so you see, you are not alone. Don't give up!

Wilma and Barbara G.

The list had about two hundred names on it, and Riley read each and every syllable. Each name warmed his heart a little more; each one strengthened his resolve a little further. The tickle next to his heart seemed to heat up, then blossom into full-blown hope; by the time he read the last name on the list, he felt as though he could bend the bars around him with his bare hands.

"Thank you," he whispered in the dark to Wilma and Barbara G. *Thank you.*

Chapter Ten

Mike the reporter had never had a story as big as this, and he took it very seriously. He'd managed to accumulate a very large nest egg selling tidbits of the Aisling story to the tabloids. His seriousness was not evident to his colleagues, since he was well known as the original prankster. He laughed too freely, and announced on nearly an hourly basis that he loved his job. They often wondered if Mike had the balls or the smarts to pursue a story to its fullest extent, considering his favorite food was *Froot Loops* and his favorite TV show *The Simpsons*.

There was a great deal they didn't know.

Like, he had a cousin who belonged to the Galactic Brethren. This cousin had just been summoned for jury duty.

Like, he followed the lead investigator in this case wherever she went.

Like, he was keeping tabs on Hagan Lamont and his team.

Whether his tactics were legal was not his concern. Whether they resulted in his story plastered on the front page *was*. Playing the innocuous goofball was just another way to maintain his edge.

He had followed Detective Casey to a dive called *The Chameleon Lounge*. The place had an old-fashioned animated neon sign: A neon chameleon shot out its neon tongue to snag a delicious, cold frosty neon beer, only to rediscover its neon thirst moments later. Music thumped inside.

He followed her inside and played Mortal Kombat while he watched her question most of the patrons and all of the staff, though each query was answered with a shake of the head. One of the patrons, a small, balding man, offered to buy her a beer, but she declined in a very ladylike way.

Before she headed for the exit, Detective Casey apparently changed her mind and indulged in a shot of Sambuca. She was just within earshot of the arcade game.

"Hey, thanks," she said to the bartender, and slid a fifty across the bar as she licked the rim of the shot glass. "Ever seen this lady in here?" Mike saw that Casey had a picture of the victim and was offering it to the bartender, who squinted through the smoke for about a minute before nodding.

"Yep. She was here about twice a week, maybe more sometimes. She was one of Jake Fry's. Ain't she that lady that got herself kilt?"

"Yep and nope. She got kilt, but not by herself." Mike almost chuckled at this; the bartender was obviously a great deal denser than the drinks he mixed. "How can I find this Jake Fry?"

"Dunno. Used to bartend here until around three-thirty or four in the morning. He quit about three weeks ago. We don' really keep records 'round here. I don't have his phone number or nothing." Casey thanked Mr. Genius and headed for the exit just as the video game ran out of quarters. He began to follow, almost on Casey's heels.

Once outside, though, Mike found he had lost his target. The detective had disappeared into the night. He approached her vehicle and scratched his head when he found it empty. "Astonishing," he remarked to himself. He had barely taken his eyes off her.

"Aren't I, though?" said a voice behind him, and all at once his arms were seized in an iron grip. The fingers around his wrists squeezed painfully until he gasped. "Who are you?"

Mike groaned inwardly, but he was also impressed.

Casey had known all along that she was being followed, just as any competent cop would. "I'm a reporter," he grunted, trying to remain still so his shoulders didn't creak. "There's ID in my coat."

"What do you know about this case?"

"Quite a lot."

"Do you know Jake Fry?"

"No."

He was released at last. "I want you to go away," Casey said severely, "and I want you to stay away. Got it?"

Mike shook his head. "No way," he said. "I'm not interfering with your investigation. I have every right to report on this story."

"Really. Are you willing to spend the night in jail for your right to report on this story?"

"Come on, Detective. Maybe we can help each other."

Detective Casey grabbed him by the front of his jacket. Her posture had changed from annoyed disinterest to one of annoyed attention. "If you have information relating to this investigation, I suggest you tell me what it is. Now."

Mike found himself a little frightened, but more than a little horny. Since boyhood, he'd cast his fantasies with Wonder Woman, She-Hulk, Mrs. Columbo, and Red Sonja. Despite his fear, or even because of it, he now thought it entirely possible that he was already in love with Detective Hilde Casey. "Okay, okay! I'll tell you what I know. We members of the media have a different spin on things."

"To say the least," Casey muttered. "Get in the car."

Jim and Patty Harrison were all-American types. He had been in the military; she had won a beauty contest. Now, they sat looking at Lamont with anything but all-American smiles.

He could almost feel rage and disgust radiating across his desk from the both of them. It made him feel hot and a bit unwell. "Thank you for coming," he ventured.

"Let's get it over with," Jim Harrison almost growled.

It wasn't their fault; they were merely responding in an emotional way because they were speaking to their daughter's killer's defense lawyer. Lamont's reputation for getting murderers off certainly couldn't help matters. At least his office was comfortable and clean, large and well stocked. He rose and poured each of them a brandy.

"Tell me about Riley," Lamont suggested as he set the drinks before them. "Tell me what he was like when you first met him, and what Alice loved about him."

"I don't know what she saw in him, actually," Patty Harrison said. She picked up her glass and took a hearty gulp. She was squeezing a handkerchief in one hand. "She could have had any man she wanted."

And she did, Lamont thought. He took a sip of brandy. "I'm sure that's true," he said. "Do you know of any problems the two of them may have been having?"

"The problem was Riley himself," Jim said. "Alice found within a very short time that she had married someone she could not respect."

"Why was that?" Lamont asked, knowing full well what Mr. Harrison's answer would be.

"He never stood up for himself, or for his wife."

"Can you be more specific, sir?"

"Little things at first—accepting poor service without complaint, working at that damn garage for ten years without a raise, ducking out of any argument he had with Alice." Mr. Harrison shook his head and then drained his glass.

In that gesture, Lamont saw volumes. He knew in an instant that Jim Harrison had never accepted poor service without complaint, expected a quarterly raise, and often started arguments just for the sake of arguing. Jim Harrison was an aristocrat.

Lamont felt a tiny burst of kinship for the man. Very tiny though—Harrison had no taste at all. *Those citrine cufflinks are downright gaudy—and come on, Old Spice?*

Patty Harrison dabbed at her eyes with the handkerchief. "Tell him about the anniversary dinner," she said. "Our poor

Alice. I never would have guessed that Riley had a temper like that."

"That has yet to be proven," Lamont reminded gently.

"I need a smoke," Jim Harrison said. "Let's go outside and I'll tell you the damn story while I have a cigarette. Stay here, Patty, okay?"

His wife looked doubtful, but she nodded.

They went out of the office and down the carpeted hall. "There's a courtyard just here on our right," Lamont said.

The small courtyard had two benches facing each other. Jim Harrison sat on one, Lamont on the other. The bare trees and shrubs surrounding them almost demanded serenity.

"Cigarette?"

"No, thanks, I quit years ago."

"We were all going out for dinner," Mr. Harrison began, drawing deeply on the cigarette, "because it was Riley and Alice's first anniversary. We still hadn't accepted that our daughter had married someone so ill suited for her, but we were concealing it so we wouldn't hurt her. Truthfully, I despised the mongrel."

It was breezy, but not windy. The cool air carrying Harrison's voice had a sharp edge to it. Lamont shivered on the shady concrete bench.

"We had reservations at the nicest restaurant in town, *Daven's*. Do you know it?"

"I know it."

"Well, we met the kids there around seven, and we could tell there was tension. You know, between the two of them? They'd obviously been fighting before they arrived."

Lamont got out his notebook and started writing. "Uh huh," he said.

"Well, our table wasn't quite ready, so we went to the lounge for a few drinks first. It's a nice lounge. We sat by the fire and listened to music and talked about the weather and Alice's new job. That's when it happened."

"What?"

"A man came over and hit on Alice. I mean, subtlety was

not in this man's vocabulary. He came over, told Alice she was a gorgeous woman. He wanted to buy her a drink."

"Then what happened?"

"Well, Alice sat there for a moment, looking to her husband to speak up, but he never did. He never even looked up from the fire, so she went with the man to the bar!" Mr. Harrison shook his head and ground the cigarette under one heel. "Alice was testing him, you see? He failed the test."

"So it was up to Riley to tell this guy to bug off?" Lamont said.

"Maybe not entirely, but he didn't say a word! He pretended not to notice! When Alice finally joined us at the dinner table an hour later, I could see it in her face. She was disappointed in her husband." Harrison got up and started walking around the bench.

"Why didn't Alice just leave Riley? Why didn't she file for divorce?"

The cigarettes came out again. The lighter. "Alice wasn't one to admit when she was wrong, especially when she felt any kind of pressure or scrutiny from her family and friends. I'm sure she wanted to stay married to prove she'd made a good choice."

Lamont nodded thoughtfully. "Are you saying that Alice's affairs go back as far as that?"

"Maybe not that far, but far. After that night, Alice knew she could do pretty much whatever she wanted. The less Riley reacted, the more she tried to get a reaction. You get me?"

But the more his wife tried to get a reaction, the less Riley would react, thought Lamont.

"Why do you think Riley reacted this time, Mr. Harrison? Why do you think he killed your daughter?"

Jim Harrison stopped walking around the bench and sat down on it. He leaned forward. Lamont met his eye. The man was weeping silently.

"He snapped," Harrison said, with not a single quiver in his voice. "No one can be a robot all their lives. It's not healthy."

Chapter Eleven

_____

The interrogation room was beginning to feel like an old friend. Lamont slipped his shoes off under the table as Riley was brought in and seated across from him as usual. There would be no questions and answers today—no rehearsing or note taking.

Seconds, then minutes flowed by as both men sat in silence, heads bowed, contemplating the difficult day ahead. There were sounds outside the room: An airplane's distant buzz. Barking dog. A ringing telephone answered.

Lamont could hear his gold watch ticking over all of it.

"Nervous?" he asked at last.

"Yes," Riley replied a moment later. His voice was barely above a whisper.

"Ready, kid?"

"Not really."

"Let's do it."

Almost before he knew it, Lamont found himself seated at the front of a packed courtroom. Two weeks had passed like two hours, and now here he sat, enjoying the rich scent of aged wood and the way the tiniest sound bounced around the ornate courtroom.

Riley was scared sick. It was as though he had dreamed

the past two weeks, and was now awakened in a tiger's deadly grip. Lamont had prepared him well for the trial, right down to appropriate facial expressions; all the same, nausea flirted shamelessly. The jury was impassive, but they watched him carefully, and worst of all, Alice's parents stared from the first row—Patty tearful and tense, Jim baleful and tense.

As prosecutor Andreana Keene shuffled papers, then rose to deliver her opening statement, he met the eye of the judge. It was cold in there, cold and blue and impenetrable. Chilled to the bone, Riley shivered and dropped his eyes.

Hagan Lamont saw his client shiver and look down at the floor, and he didn't blame him. Judge Dempster was very menacing, very imposing and very detached. The man possessed the scariest, iciest eyes this side of Mars beneath lightning bolt brows and would not suffer incompetence or contempt.

Most judges projected authority on the bench. Judge Dempster was authority incarnate.

"Ladies and gentlemen, over these next weeks, you will become embroiled in a tragic story," Keene began, her voice spotless and bright, "and the conclusion of this story will be determined by your very selves. As you learn about this story, you are going to feel sorry for the man sitting over there—the defendant. Truly, Riley Aisling is as much the victim of tragedy as he is the cause of it! To top it off, he really looks the part.

"The matter before us, however, is this: Did this man resort to murder when a simple divorce would have sufficed?" Keene paused and turned to look Riley in the eye; as Lamont could have predicted, the jury followed suite. He recognized the method and its effect. Keene was trying to make Riley squirm for the jury. To his credit, he remained perfectly motionless.

Unfortunately, he also paled and began to cry. Lamont cringed inside; suddenly he felt like crying himself. How many times had he said it in the last fourteen days? *Don't concentrate on the bitchy D.A. Keep your focus on the jury. Stay conscious of them and what they might be thinking.* He'd said it to his client a hundred times at least. Keene turned her smug face back to the jury.

"The People will prove, beyond a shadow of a doubt, that this man is guilty of the crime of murder. You will learn to look past your pity and compassion to the cold heart of the matter: The defendant broke the law. He killed a human being." Keene placed her self-satisfied ass back in her chair.

Yeah. He killed Hagan Lamont, high-power attorney. Farewell, you handsome devil.

"The Assistant D.A. over there wants you to look past your pity and compassion, and I must say, that's good advice. Without those emotions, you will have to rely on evidence.

"The evidence clearly shows that Riley Aisling's wife was indeed murdered. But it does not prove beyond Ms. Keene's 'shadow of a doubt' that my client was the one who perpetrated the terrible act." Lamont conjured a sad smile for the six men and six women in the jury box. He shook his head and asked *Can you believe it?* with his eyes. He knew without looking that Riley would be crying again by now, which would work to their advantage this time. *Eat this, toots! I have my own ways of getting to a jury!* "In fact, there is no actual evidence that even suggests it. This is another in a string of tragedies that seem to overwhelm my client on a consistent basis. Ms. Keene said it herself: Riley Aisling is a victim. He is not a killer. Thank you."

The media stirred at the back of the courtroom, as they always did when there was a lull. Lamont looked closely as he returned to his chair; it seemed Riley's story had triumphed over the ocean, only to attract more and more sharks as it plowed through salty distances. He thought he saw a Canadian news sticker on one of those microphones—and there, wasn't that a BBC logo?

Andreana Keene began by calling neighbors from the houses on either side of Junie's. Lamont knew from the witness list that there were four neighbors who would be called, and each one remembered hearing Riley yelling at Alice, calling her a whore. Each of them also remembered hearing Alice's screams. "Have you ever heard anything like you heard that night?" Keene asked witness number four. Witness number four was the man from the house on the left of Junie's.

"Never. It sounded awful. It sounded like they wanted to kill each other."

"Objection," Lamont said. Judge Dempster was already nodding.

"Sustained. The jury will disregard."

Keene passed Lamont on the way back to her chair; he noticed she smelled faintly of lemons. He stood. "Mr. Alexander, if the fight sounded so serious, why did you not call the police?"

"I did! The storm delayed the cops."

Lamont preened for a moment before continuing his cross in earnest; it was something he did while he thought. He assumed long ago that he'd adopted the habit from his mother, Lucy Lamont, Webster's definition for dignified. "Mr. Alexander," he said, "have you ever had a fight with your wife?"

"Of course."

"You've yelled at each other, called each other names?"

"Well, yes, but…"

"And were you ever worried about what the neighbors might think if they heard you?"

Mr. Alexander was about thirty-five, with harried little pig eyes. "Yes," he said. "I suppose so."

"What's the worst thing you've ever said to your wife during a fight?"

"Objection," Keene said. "Relevance."

"Your Honor, not everyone who calls their wife a terrible name ends up killing her."

"Overruled. The witness will answer."

Mr. Alexander took a deep breath and flush red right to the roots of his hair. "I called her a fat nagging bitch one time. I never forgave myself."

"Thank you, Mr. Alexander. You may step down."

Keene had very nice legs, Lamont noticed—not for the first time—as she called Officer Casey to the stand. She asked about Riley's state of mind on the night he was arrested.

"Objection!" Lamont piped up. "The witness is not a mental health expert." The judge agreed.

"Withdrawn," Keene said, with a tilt of her head, her voice too smooth. "Officer Casey, you are trained to deal with the distraught and confused, correct?"

"Yes."

"And was the defendant distraught or confused when you arrested him?"

"Yes, he was."

Keene had no more questions, so Lamont rose and asked if Riley had any blood on him at the time of the arrest? When she responded in the negative, Lamont produced his most charming smile and asked if Riley had resisted arrest, or tried to flee? Again, the cop responded no.

"And, in your considered opinion, what was his demeanor?"

"He seemed confused, disoriented, unable to get out of his vehicle."

Lamont smiled warmly. "No further questions, your Honor."

Next on Keene's roster was the medical examiner, who testified to the cause and time of death.

"Bludgeoned with the telephone, strangled with the telephone cord, between 4 and 5 am. The defendant's semen was present in the victim's body."

Lamont rolled his eyes and stood as Keene sat. He knew he was swaggering a bit, but couldn't help it. He loved refuting circumstantial evidence almost as much as Keene loved to use it to sway a jury. "Doctor Cunnings," he said, "you've proven admirably something we already knew—that my client visited, and had sex with his wife. Now, what medical evidence do you have that directly ties Riley Aisling to the murder? DNA, blood evidence, tissue?"

Cunnings cleared his throat, and Lamont was instantly

on guard. Had Keene predicted this line of questioning? And did she have an ace up her sleeve in the form of some damning physical evidence? Well, better to call her bluff now than allow her to up the stakes!

"Well, none, really," Cunnings was saying. "Except for the semen, a few hairs, and the fingerprints lifted from the home."

Lamont quietly exhaled. "Thank you, Doctor, that's all."

Next, Keene called Sergeant Ernie Jackson, who testified how the cops had found Riley's fingerprints throughout Junie's house, and on the murder weapon.

"Who found Mrs. Aisling's body?" Keene inquired as she looked knowingly at the jury.

"The police. We were called by the neighbors."

"Did you find anything in the house that might have angered Mr. Aisling, may have led to the fight?"

"Objection. Counsel is leading the witness."

"Sustained. Rephrase your question, Ms. Keene."

Keene paused briefly. "During your search of the house, did you find an answering machine?"

"Yes."

"And did you listen to the messages on the machine?"

"Yes."

"Please tell the Court and the jury what you heard."

"An unidentified man was arranging to meet Mrs. Aisling. From the content of the message, it was obvious they had a romantic liaison planned."

"Was Mr. Aisling aware of this message?"

"According to a statement given by Mr. Aisling immediately following his arrest, he heard the message, and was enraged."

"And what was the time stamp on the message?"

"Four a.m."

There was a hush in the courtroom and Keene let the damaging information sink in for a minute or two before she continued. Lamont admired her technique.

"Was there any blood evidence at the scene? And if so, please explain to us what you concluded from your analysis."

Jackson nodded. "The blood was spattered upwards, in an arc on the ceiling and walls. This indicates that the murder weapon, the phone, was raised over and over again, as the killer struck the victim's skull," he said gesturing. One of the jurors, a middle-age woman, gasped.

"The murderer apparently was small of stature, and had to raise his arm high to build up enough power to kill the victim."

Lamont noticed that all of the jurors suddenly had their eyes trained on his client, who was slight in build.

"Also, repeated blows were necessary to kill her."

"The State would like to submit the following crime scene photographs into evidence, Your Honor," Keene said, approaching the bench. "They graphically illustrate the brutal nature of the crime."

Judge Dempster glanced at the photographs and closed his eyes for a moment before passing them to the jury via a bailiff. Lamont knew he would have to counter quickly; shocking photos had unexpected effects on juries.

"Is there any possibility that someone else might have killed Mrs. Aisling?" Lamont asked as he approached the witness stand.

Jackson replied impassively. "Anything's possible. But we believe we've done a thorough investigation and have made a proper arrest. As to the defendant's guilt, Mr. Aisling is innocent until proven guilty. It's not our job to presume innocence or guilt." *He was probably lying through his teeth, but it was a good answer!*

Satisfied, Lamont sat as Keene called Junie to the stand.

"How well do you know the defendant, Ms. Harrison?"

"Pretty well. He and I were in elementary school and high school together."

"You lived in the same neighborhood?"

"No. Riley and his folks lived on the Curve."

"The Curve?"

Junie looked at her nails. "The Curve is the part of town where the disadvantaged live."

"Very politically correct," Lamont said under his breath. Riley nodded. He had told Lamont in one of a million depositions that his parents were not disadvantaged; they were dirt poor. His dad liked to gamble and drink and smoke weed—expensive habits. By the time Riley was old enough to get a job, he was paying all the bills and buying most of the food. Naturally, his mother was forbidden from working. It was a far cry from Lamont's own privileged and uneventful childhood.

"Did Riley ever come to school with bruises on his body?" Keene wanted to know. She was pacing slowly between the jury box and her chair.

"All the time," Junie responded to the prosecutor. "But the bruises weren't the worst of it. Riley's dad liked to play mind games. He liked to keep Riley on his toes, liked to stay unpredictable. He was a real bully."

"Unpredictable and violent?"

"Yes."

"Do you know if Riley witnessed violence at home? Did he see any sort of domestic violence?"

"Oh, yes, daily" Junie said softly, "right up to the end."

Why you sneaky... Lamont could see Keene's next question coming like spring after winter: "The end? Explain that."

He was already on his feet. "Your Honor! Objection! May we approach?"

Keene had a smirk on her round face as she joined him before the judge. "What now, Lamont? The truth hurt?"

He ignored her. "Your honor, any revelations the prosecution wish to make about my client's past would be irrelevant and extremely prejudicial. I move to suppress."

"Your Honor," Keene countered, "Aisling's past provides direct proof of his guilt, based on learned behavior. I can bring a dozen shrinks before the court to attest to the validity of..."

"Counselors, please!" He only whispered, and his eyes remained fixed on his paperwork, but they knew better than to keep arguing. "I'll take your motion under advisement, Counselor," Dempster continued. "Until I have a chance to review your motion, the objection is sustained." He swung his stern, white head toward the jury. "The jury will disregard any previous mention of the defendant's childhood history as a victim of domestic violence," he instructed. Lamont felt the vibes in the room shift as the judge abandoned his whisper. "Proceed, Ms. Keene."

"Only one more question. Ms. Harrison, would you describe your sister's marriage to Mr. Aisling as happy?"

Junie shook her head slowly. "No. My sister was planning to divorce Riley."

"Thank you. Your witness."

Lamont gave Keene a smile as she returned to her seat; she arched an eyebrow and looked away. *Bitchy, bitchy!* He rose. "Ms. Harrison, do you like the defendant?"

"Yes. I've always been fond of him."

"Do you believe him capable of this crime?"

Utter silence reigned as Junie considered her answer. Lamont saw that Riley Aisling was holding his breath and wondered why Junie's answer held so much importance for him. "No," Junie said at last. "Riley wouldn't hurt a fly."

The gavel rose and fell as Judge Dempster, apparently hungry, adjourned the court until the next day. The press, who had been remarkably well behaved during the proceedings, clamored and danced at the back of the courtroom.

"Hang in there, Riley," Lamont said into his client's ear as he was taken back to his cell. "This roller coaster is just warming up."

Chapter Twelve

Vi and Harry Langhofer were waiting in the comfortable chairs outside his office when Lamont arrived, his briefcase heavier with each passing second. He knew why they were there, and groaning inwardly, Lamont gave them a nod. They rose as he approached.

"Mr. Lamont, why have we not received notice that we are to testify on Riley's behalf?" Harry asked, following close behind as Lamont unlocked the door and entered his office.

"Sir, I'm sorry, but your testimony is not what Riley needs. He needs the jury to believe him. If he were pleading not guilty for reason of insanity, your testimony would be very helpful, but he's not. Do you understand?"

Vi had come into the office and was standing at one of the enormous windows, looking out at the night. "We only want to help Riley," she said.

Lamont joined her at the window and put his hand on her shoulder. "I know you do," he said softly. "Be there for him, keep his spirits up. That's the only way you can help him right now."

Hilde Casey had a suspicion that the bartender had lied when she had asked him about Jake Fry. Her gut told her that he knew Fry, and was covering for him. She stocked her car for a stakeout and settled in with her favorite music. Living in her car for days on end was nothing new to her; it reminded her of fishing with her father. Be patient, her father always said, and you'll get a nibble, or a chomp. Let the bobber float. She watched *The Chameleon Lounge* tirelessly; it was her bobber, the anchor that held the hook and the bait in place.

There was something new about this operation though—Mike. The last thing Hilde wanted was for awkward splashing to scare the fish away. So here he sat, incredibly, in the passenger seat, reading comic books and eating Pop Rocks with noisy abandon.

"Quiet," she snapped.

"Man," he said, swallowing thickly, "you're uptight."

"Maybe."

"No, you are. But I'm sure aloofness has worked for you in the past, huh."

"I suppose."

They sat in silence for a moment, and then he asked, "Is it hard doing what you do, looking the way you do? Is it harder than for other... detectives?"

"What is this, a Barbara Walters interview?"

"Just trying to get to know you, Detective Casey." His tone was light. "You know, making conversation. Forget I spoke at all." Up came the Pop Rocks. There was silence again, except for the snapping candy, but it was comfortable, and Hilde realized that he was not going to push her to answer. She gave him a sidelong glance; he was reading *Spawn*. Something told her that the comfortable silence would not be broken until she was ready to break it. She thought about his question. It was surprisingly insightful; she had wondered about the answer herself many times.

"This job is hard no matter what you look like," she said quietly. Mike put the comic book down and looked at her. "Some days are more difficult than others, and I prefer to think my looks don't enter into the fact that I'm a hell of a cop."

Mike nodded, but didn't speak. Hilde glanced his way and found him listening intently. He wasn't faking interest, and he wasn't listening just so he could relate.

"Sometimes, people don't take me seriously because I'm a woman. Can you believe that? Even in this day and age. People like that don't care what I look like, only that I wear a bra."

Mike nodded again. *Did I just talk about my bra to this man?* "Gives you a leg up," he said, "over stupid people."

Hilde smiled. It was true, stupid people did tend to underestimate her. She glanced at him again, this time in a new light. Perhaps she had done some underestimating of her own. "So what's your story?" she asked. "You got your own leg up over stupid people?"

"Yup. But you're smart, so you already know what it is."

"How long have you been a reporter?"

"About a year. Before that I worked for National Geographic."

Hilde couldn't hide it; she was impressed. "You traveled all over, wrote articles and things?"

"Yup. Best job in the world."

"So why did you leave?"

Mike smiled and looked her in the eye. "Loneliest job in the world, too. Kind of like homicide detective."

The comfortable silence returned. Hilde thought about Mike at the top of a mountain or in the middle of a rainforest or conversing with African Bushmen. Then she pictured him with a supply of Pop Rocks and actually giggled.

"What a sound!" Mike exclaimed. "I hope I hear a lot more of it."

Of course this was her cue to freeze up again, at least a little.

"What do you know about Aisling?" she asked. "The name seems really familiar to me, but there's nothing on him in the database."

Mike closed the comic book and put it down. "Are you serious?" he said. "That guy was the center of a media circus once before, about fifteen years ago. He's probably not in your database because he was a minor at the time."

Aisling… Aisling… Wait. What was tweaking her memory? "Tell me more," Hilde said.

Chapter Thirteen

After the stress of the media and the crowded courtroom, Riley found himself both relieved and contented to be back in his cell. It was blissfully dark, blissfully quiet, and for the first time since his arrival, Sleep beckoned with a shapely finger.

The clock in the hall ticks louder at night that it does during the day. It must, because Riley has never heard it ticking before now. Daddy is snoring like a dragon, though, and as long as he hears that cavernous *Quaaannh*, he knows he is safe. He has stuffed a backpack with carefully considered supplies, not an easy feat with one arm—the left—in a cast and sling. It took him weeks to gather the items and hide them from Daddy; now Riley smiles as he lifts the backpack and feels its weight. It sits easily on his back.

Carefully, carefully! Riley tiptoes down the hallway. His mother, true to her word, has left the bedroom door open a crack. The cavernous *Quaaannh* is much louder now, and a thrill of fear runs up his arms and ripples his scalp as he pushes open the door to the monster's den. His mother is already standing beside the bed, a statue in the dark. She sees him and gives a tiny, terrified wave. He waves back with his good arm, then backs slowly out of the room, never taking his eyes off his mother.

She starts her escape, footsteps timed to coincide with the dragon's snore. Her face gleams bone-white, a ghostly visage in the night. She holds her hands out in front of her, like the Mummy or Frankenstein's monster. *Quaaannh.* Riley can see she is holding her breath. One step, then two, then three. Riley feels a burst of pride; he holds his hand out to this woman who he hardly knows, yet loves with all his heart. Four, five. *Quaaannh.* The minutes tick by as she comes nearer and nearer to the door, and the dragon snores on. Her pale face is wet with tears. Riley vows this will be the very last time he will ever see a tear on his mom's face. *Quaaannh.* Six, seven, and her cold, thin fingers are in his.

Her smile is wide and joyful, but her eyes are pools of dread. Riley knows they must go *now*, he squeezes her fingers and starts to tug her gently toward the outside world. She follows willingly, but can't resist a glance toward the open bedroom door. He shakes his head at her, anxious of the slightest disturbance in the very air around them. *What are you doing, Mom? Don't you know he can feel your eyes? Don't you know he can smell your blood and hear your heartbeat and sense what you are thinking?* The hallway clock still ticks with its unnatural loudness, but now, Riley's heart lurches painfully as he suddenly realizes: The snoring has stopped.

Panic whispers in his ear, "The dragon is awake."

A hulking nightmare, his father stands in the bedroom doorway. "You little bastard," he growls, his diseased voice darker than the deepest black. "I knew it. I goddamn *know* it."

Riley's mom has taken a step forward, holding her hands over her head like a Prisoner of War. They rehearsed what they would say if they were caught, but her lines seem to have expired in her throat. Her mouth opens and closes soundlessly.

"Nothing to say, bitch?" A monster released from his cage, Daddy is coming out of the doorway. He is holding his belt, folded in two, like a weapon, in his right fist. It is so very dark;

only the streetlights outside streak the room with watery light. Riley is glad he can't see the grotesque expression on his dad's face; he can imagine it, though, and that is enough. Lips pulled back tight into a snarl, Daddy's eyes roll and shine in his head. The hallway clock ticks on like nothing is about to happen.

"Come here." Such is the terrible power of that black voice that his mother actually takes a few steps. Riley shoots a hand out to clasp her elbow.

"Mom, no. Don't. We should go, now."

She stops, but reluctantly. His father can't believe his eyes. "Oh, are you the man of the house, now?" He advances until he is a few feet away, and then stops, as though there is a wall between them. He paces back and forth, growling. "Do I not put a roof over your head and food in your belly? I am the man of this house, boy, and I'm very surprised you would forget that. Now *come here*." These last words are spoken to Mom, but Riley squeezes her elbow harder. The wall his father has built between them seems to be providing some protection. Perhaps, Riley thinks, I have found his weakness.

Riley straightens his spine and looks his father directly in his rolling eyes. There is madness there, yes, and evil. But there is something new as well. Fear—a dictator's fear of being overthrown. Riley takes a deep breath and says the one word he has never dared utter to his father:

Riley says, "No."

Just as he hopes, Dad is staggered—he doesn't move as Riley pulls his mother toward the door. The only sound is the steady, inexorable tick-tock of the hallway clock.

Then, a sound, starting out as a low rumble, drowns out the ticking of time. The sound builds until it explodes into a roar; the sound is pure fury itself. Riley is only fifteen and he has made a fatal error. The monster is enraged.

With a snarl, it leaps upon them with heart-stopping speed and sinks its claws into his mother's throat. Riley throws himself upon the big man, but, with the quickness of a snake, his father picks him up and literally throws him across the room.

The end table breaks under his weight; a broken lamp carves the flesh on his outer thigh. Pain explodes around him in a paralyzing detonation as a few ribs snap. His broken arm, bent under him, is a sausage stuffed with broken glass. The table pushes hard into his lower back.

His eyes are only shut for a few seconds; when he opens them, his father has slipped the belt around Mommy's neck and is standing behind her with his knee in her back. He's pulling at the belt with both hands. Mommy is fighting weakly, but she's a tiny woman. He switches the belt easily to one hand and reaches around to squeeze her breast with the other as she suffers defeat. He whispers something in her ear, but Riley doesn't want to hear! *I can't hear her breathing... Her tongue is a black balloon...*

"This is your fault, boy," the monster growls, shaking his mother's body. Her arms and legs are limp and toneless, like they're full of water. "You broke the rules. You tried to take her away. You really screwed up royally this time."

Riley started awake to the sound of his own cry echoing around the cell. His body was chilled to the very bone, his stomach a hot knot at the center of it. Fading quickly, the nightmare left a menacing stain in the air over his cot that wouldn't let him sleep. *I haven't thought about that night in years...*

He drew his knees to his chest and stared out at the stars until Hagan Lamont called much later that night.

Chapter Fourteen

Daven's was crowded for a Tuesday. Since he always ate light when he was in court, Lamont ordered a Thai salad, chock full of brain food. Victor and Kathleen had already ordered. Lamont checked a shiny butter knife for any signs of overt smugness on his face. He always felt cocky and invincible after a productive court day. "So, what news?" he inquired.

Kathleen checked her notes. "Well, there is still very limited forensic evidence that Aisling committed this crime." She passed a paper to Lamont. "That's a good thing. I just got this from the judge, not a good thing."

The judge had decided not to uphold Lamont's motion to suppress. The prosecution would be allowed to present Riley's past as part of their evidence.

"Ridiculous!" Lamont huffed. "It's the old crimes of the father argument. Not to mention nature versus nurture. If the jury finds out what a demon Riley's father was…"

"Maybe you can still convince him to change his plea and take the insanity defense."

Lamont shook his head. There was no way Riley was going to back down on his alibi story. "No easy way out here," he said, "especially when the client won't do what's best for him."

Victor took off his glasses and polished them with a silk napkin. "Uh... There's more. Dr. Walker got the results back on that piece of metal that was found inside Aisling's nose."

"And?"

"Well, it can't be identified. No one is really sure what it's made of, or where it came from. The Doc said the lab dulled three diamond drill bits trying to get a sample of the damn thing under a microscope."

Lamont took several swallows of his icy water and felt his stomach freezing over. "Creepy."

"Yeah."

"What does it mean?"

"Uh..." Victor was sweating, a rare bodily function for him. "In itself, maybe it means the lab is full of morons, or Aisling somehow got his hands on a very rare piece of metal. But there's more."

Lamont drank more water. Where was his salad? He looked around for the waiter. "More? Like what?"

"Here. I've drafted a report," Vic said, passing the sheaf to Lamont, "but suffice it to say, maybe we should rethink things."

Hagan Lamont, safe in his cozy world of cut-and-dry law and Thai salads and gold-plated prestige, read the report, which was all about his client's insides. With each word he read, his cozy world seemed to shrink away more and more, until it was a single huge, cold needle, on which he perched, trying desperately to keep his balance on the sharp point, unable to escape to a safe surface. The cold water in his belly rippled.

The air was gone from his lungs, but try as he might, Lamont could not draw fresh breath. Was his staff enjoying his rare speechlessness and bewilderment? No. They shared it. He stared at them in turn, and his mouth hung open unconsciously.

The food arrived, but he pushed the salad away with numb fingers. Hagan Lamont wondered again what it was like to be crazy. It probably felt a lot like this. There was only one thing that could be said, and he said it: "Holy Shit."

Kathleen nodded. "Yeah," she said, "you can say that again."

Lamont slept not a wink that night; he didn't even bother turning down the bed. All he could do was look out at the night, to look out at those stars, and ask himself if all he'd ever believed, and chosen not to believe, summed up to a speck of dust in all that cosmos. Though he'd consulted beloved friends like Johnny Walker, Jim Beam, and good ole' Jack, he knew there was only one person in the Universe who could help him.

Riley's voice seemed to reflect the ageless weariness of the stars themselves; how long had it been since he slept? "Hello." There was an edge to the somnolent voice, and Lamont recognized it all too easily: Distrust.

"It seems I owe you an apology," he said.

Chapter Fifteen

Hilde Casey walked around her car, stretching her legs and thinking. Mike had dozed off about half an hour ago, and to keep from falling asleep herself, she had left the car.

The slight exercise woke her brain quickly. Aisling... Aisling... now that she had a chance to ponder, she was certain her memory would cooperate...

Aisling...

Oh my God...

She remembered. When Hilde had first become a cop, she had worked her first homicide only a couple of months out of the academy. Aisling had been the name of the victim. That woman had followed her around for years. She'd been an awful sight: Tongue black, eyes bulging, blood covering her face and hands. Every so often, Hilde would turn from a routine task, like laundry or target practice, and there she'd be, just for a second, before a blink or on the edge of a sneeze.

Her radio crackled inside the car. Mike snorted loudly and awoke. She hurried to answer the call. "Yeah."

"We have a description for you, Detective, on that name you gave us."

Hilde met Mike's eye and saw her own smile. "Finally! And?"

"Jake Fry has a long rap sheet—assault, possession, and B&E, mostly. He's five-two, balding, wiry."

The man, the man who had offered to buy her a beer! Unbelievable. Mike was nodding; he'd also made the connection. At least now she knew what she was fishing for. "Thanks, Louise. Gotta go."

Mike wiped spittle from his cheek and stretched. Then he put a hand on the door handle. "Ready?"

Hilde frowned. "What? Are you nuts?"

"Aren't we going in?"

"No, we are not. Sudden movements scatter the fish."

Mike was silent for a moment. "Okay," he said.

He didn't argue.

He didn't try to persuade.

He didn't make a break for it.

Mike just said, "Okay."

"You agree we should stay in the car?" she asked, puzzled. In the course of so many hours together, and so many conversations, Hilde had gleaned from his body language that he was relaxed, non-confrontational, and that he'd yet to tell so much as a tiny white lie. She had never met a man less threatened by her. It was marvelous.

"My job's very important. But yours is more important, and you do it well."

"Thanks."

"Can I tell you something?"

"Okay…"

"I am very attracted to you."

Hilde smiled. "I'm attracted to your honesty."

"Yeah?"

"Yes. It's the deepest part of anyone I've been attracted to in a very long time. Do you think we could hold on the physical for a while?"

Mike smiled back at her and took her hand. Hilde thought he was going to kiss it, but instead he smelled it. His nose just grazed the surface of her skin as he inhaled deeply, his eyes closed and his forehead smooth. Then he looked up into her eyes.

"We can hold on the physical forever if it's what you want."

"Forever? No. But for once, I want other things from a man."

"You'll get them."

"I believe you."

They were back in the courtroom, and despite his turbulent night, Lamont did not allow the jury to see his shaken, sleepless side. Although he had purple smudges under his eyes, he was still as crisp as celery to them. Riley, on the other hand, seemed more relaxed than ever before, even though he was scheduled to testify today.

Though he was still anxious and afraid, Riley projected an inner peace that had not been present before.

Keene seemed to sense this, and Lamont heard her use her surliest tone as she recalled Junie to the stand.

"I remind you that you are still under oath."

Junie only nodded.

"Ms. Harrison, do you remember my question yesterday? You said that you believed that the defendant had witnessed violence at home right up until the end. Please explain what you meant by that."

"All right." Junie took a deep breath and looked to Riley. Their eyes met and Lamont felt something pass between them.

"About fifteen years ago, there was a murder here in Left Ridge. A man beat and choked his wife into a coma. She remained unconscious for about three months, then died."

Keene nodded. "Go on."

"Well, it made all the papers, and their only son, well, that was Riley. He saw the whole thing. He was fifteen years old."

Junie couldn't look at Riley anymore. Instead she looked at her nails. Lamont saw that the media was abuzz at the back of the courtroom, but the gavel rose and fell, and all was silent once again.

"So," Keene continued, "the defendant grew up witnessing violent acts against women, particularly his own mother, then he was too scared to testify against his own father when his mother was murdered."

Junie didn't answer. Her mind was in the past.

"Ms. Harrison?"

"Yes. That's what happened."

"And after this… this incident, when Riley was placed into foster care, did you remain in contact with him?"

"Yes."

"Thank you. I have no more questions for this witness, Judge."

Dempster gave Junie a moment, then said, "You may step down."

"Next she's calling the shrink who examined you after the death of your mother," Lamont said into Riley's ear, "but don't worry. I know just how to handle it."

The child psychologist was small, blond, and bland. He wore a trim mustache, which was graying at the edges, and a trim smile. "Doctor Kornelson, what is the usual effect of long-term exposure to violence at an early age?"

Lamont found the doctor's voice as bland as the rest of him. "Statistics show that children, male children in particular, who have been exposed to long-term domestic violence have a seventy-eight percent chance of becoming abusers themselves. However, that statistic does not apply to youngsters who have received extensive counseling. The recidivism rate is significantly lower in those cases."

"Was Riley Aisling placed into therapy after the death of his mother?"

"Only for a short mandatory period."

"Do you know why counseling was not continued?"

"No. It was recommended, but for some reason, Riley did not receive any follow up care."

"Thank you, Doctor. I have no more questions."

Lamont cracked his knuckles noisily before standing.

"Doctor Kornelson, when you examined young Riley, did you find any evidence that his exposure to violence created a propensity in him to repeat his father's crimes?"

"I, uh..."

Lamont interrupted, "In fact, didn't you find that the defendant had developed an extreme aversion to violence, especially against women, and feared confrontation of any kind?"

"Yes. It seemed that way."

"Seemed that way or was that way? Your report," Lamont said, holding up a stack of papers neatly stapled together, "seems to indicate that you found young Riley," he looked at the report, "and I quote, 'an unusually gentle boy, who is remarkably ready for transition into society and foster care. Counseling is suggested, not mandated.' Do you recall making this report, Doctor?"

He handed the sheaf of papers to the doctor. Dr. Kornelson examined them.

"Yes, I vaguely remember."

"Thank you, Doctor. You may step down."

Lamont sat as Andreana Keene, pouting, produced a new voice, a voice like a town crier, and it boomed around the courtroom as she pointed in Riley's direction.

"Your Honor," she said, "I call Riley Aisling to the stand."

Dempster nodded and raised a finger. "If I hear a peep from the back of my courtroom, I'll clear it so fast you'll think God Himself had a hand in it. Understood?"

There was no reply, just silent compliance.

Riley was sworn in. Lamont noticed Keene was wearing three-inch heels today.

"When did you discover your wife was having an affair, Mr. Aisling?"

"I've suspected for about a year. It was confirmed the last night we spent together. She received a call from one of her boyfriends."

"A year? Didn't that kind of... eat away at you?"

"Yes, it did," he said haltingly. "But I wasn't sure, I had to wait for evidence."

"Ah. Evidence like a tender message on the machine from your wife's boyfriend. The same message the jury heard yesterday. Is that right?"

Riley dropped his eyes.

"I'm sorry, Mr. Riley, I didn't hear your response."

"Yes, that's right."

Keene had a pen in her manicured plump right hand. She chewed it thoughtfully. "It seems to me you had plenty of time to plan a murder. Did you kill your wife, Mr. Aisling? Beat her with the telephone, strangle her into oblivion with the cord?"

Lamont nodded in encouragement. *This is it.*

Riley took a deep breath and glanced at the jury. One of the jurors looked a lot like his father. He swallowed hard. "No, ma'am, I didn't. I was not with my wife when the murder occurred."

"Convenient. Would you mind telling the court where you were, when a half dozen neighbors heard your outraged shouts, and your wife's desperate cries for help?"

"Objection!"

"Sustained. Counselor, keep the editorial to yourself, or I swear I'll hold you in contempt."

Keene's mouth twisted into the kind of smile one gives ranting street-corner maniacs. "Well, then, if you weren't present, where in the world, or should I say universe, were you, Mr. Aisling?"

Snickering broke out in the courtroom, and the judge pounded his gavel on the heavy oak.

"I know this sounds crazy, but I was abducted, taken against my will, by, by...well, I was taken by aliens. When I left the house, my wife was fine."

Like the wave at a sporting event, a mixture of gasps and giggles traveled around the courtroom. Not even the jury could maintain poker faces, concealing derision behind their hands.

Keene smirked. "Aliens, Mr. Aisling? And did these aliens also kill your wife?" Lamont sprang to his feet.

"Objection."

"Question withdrawn." Keene clasped her hands behind

her and rolled her eyes heavenward theatrically.

"Your honor, is this really a viable defense?"

The judge shrugged and looked to Lamont.

"Sir, we have every intention of presenting evidence to support my client's alibi."

"Very well. Proceed, Ms. Keene."

"Prosecution has no further questions, your honor."

"We'll continue tomorrow. Court's adjourned."

Chapter Sixteen

The story spread like a virus, from the newspapers to the television news. Even Jay Leno used Riley's defense to amuse his audience. "Why didn't O.J. think of that?" he crowed one night.

Headlines abounded: "Welcome to the Twilight Zone," and "Unbelievable Alibi Confirmed!" and "Lamont, Come Down to Earth!"

The press was merciless as well as relentless, and for once, Riley was actually grateful for his peaceful, quiet cell. Dawn came all too soon, however, and after a morning jog through the media, he was back in court.

Keene's first witness was Dr. Leonard. The old psychologist with the long lashes stepped down after about forty minutes. Lamont murmured that she had assured the jury that Riley believed what he was saying.

"He's not sociopathic," she'd said with confidence.

"Could he be lying?"

"Not in my opinion."

Keene hadn't been convinced so easily. "Isn't it true that in your original psych-social report, you diagnosed the defendant as 'delusional and possibly psychotic'?"

"Yes."

"And is that still your diagnosis?"

"No."

"So, what you're saying is, Doctor, that you believe the defendant's alibi?"

Dr. Leonard straightened her spine and locked eyes with the prosecutor.

"What I'm saying, young lady, is I cannot repudiate the defendant's claim. Nor can I dismiss Mr. Aisling's testimony. As I got to know him better, I began to realize that he wasn't delusional at all, but had experienced something terribly traumatic. Something that perhaps none of us in this courtroom will ever be able to fully understand or explain!"

Lamont had decided not to recall any of the prosecution's witnesses, since their only purpose was to glorify Keene's circumstantial evidence.

"Your Honor, I call Shane Harley, of the Galactic Brethren."

The man who took the stand was burly, and though his bald head was tattooed and his face pierced and bejeweled in a variety of locations, he wore an expensive suit and appeared anything but flaky. He was sworn in; his voice was genderless and light. As he sat, he shot a wink in Riley's direction.

"Mr. Harley," Lamont began, "isn't it true that shortly after the defendant was arrested, your organization began an investigation into his claims of abduction?"

"That's Dr. Harley. Yes, it's true. I'm a parapsychologist and ufologist."

Lamont smiled and nodded. "What did you discover about my client's experience?"

Shane Harley leaned back. "You're correct when you call it an 'experience'," he said, "because many, many people around the world have been abducted, and they mostly report similar experiences."

"Why are you so quick to believe what these people say?"

"Because," Harley said with a smile, "I, too, have been abducted. In my case, the aliens recognized an open-mindedness in me that is difficult to find on Earth. I have a relationship with them."

"Your Honor, objection!" Keene called out. "The defense is merely trying to make their client's story appear less ridiculous by introducing a tale even stranger than his!"

Dempster looked pained. "Overruled," he said, "though I sympathize."

Lamont smiled inwardly—he had just squeaked by on that one. Keene had been right. Luckily, the judge hadn't seen it that way.

Harley was shaking his head.

"Is there anything you would like to add?" Lamont asked.

"Only that I find it despicable that we, as a species, would rather implicate one of our own, put him through this horrible trial, make him fight for his life, rather than acknowledge that there is other intelligent life in the universe. Do we really know everything there is to know in the cosmos? Are we certain enough to condemn a man to death?"

"Your Honor," Keene whined.

"That's enough, Mr. Lamont," Dempster said. "This is still a murder trial. Ask your witness a relevant question, or ask him to step down."

Lamont tilted his head elegantly. "I have no further questions," he said. "I would now like to call Riley Aisling to the stand."

Riley felt warmed by a second wink from Shane Harley, and took the stand with a minimum of trembling.

"Please, tell us what happened the night your wife was murdered, Mr. Aisling."

"Well, I had planned to spend the night with my wife, at her sister's. We were trying to reconcile," he said. He paused, looking down at his clenched hands. "Then, around four, some guy called and left a message on the machine."

Lamont decided that less was more, and didn't pursue it further. The jury had already heard the tape, and the results had been devastating.

"Go on."

"Well, I was really mad. We got in a fight, and I left."

"Did you kill your wife?"

"No! I loved her. Even after everything she did…the cheating, the lying, everything."

"Fine. Go on. What did you do next?"

"I was heading back toward Left Ridge. I had been on the road about ten minutes when the engine stalled and I couldn't get it restarted. I got out of the car, and I couldn't move."

"Couldn't move, Mr. Aisling? Do you suffer from seizures?"

"No, sir. It was like I was paralyzed. I looked up and saw this light in the sky." His eyes began to fill with tears. "That's when they took me. I know it sounds crazy, but I swear to God, that's what happened."

Lamont had the jury entranced. He stared at them gravely; their serious expressions mirrored his. "I know this is hard, but you must keep going."

"They kept me for hours. I couldn't move a muscle."

"What did these, these aliens, these creatures look like?"

"They were small, grey, with big black eyes. I was on a table, naked. It was cold. They touched my body and took samples from inside and out."

Riley closed his eyes, but the tears wouldn't abate. His hands shook in his lap. *I'm the only one in this courtroom*, he told himself, *and there is no reason to hold back, no reason to stop.* The fractured images in his mind were finally materializing into a story anyone could understand.

"I was just a specimen to them, an animal to be examined, a subject with no feelings. I kept trying to stop them, but they wanted semen, they wanted urine, blood, spinal fluid, brain tissue, lung tissue, colon cells, stomach contents, lots of stuff. They were rough, their instruments were cold and hard."

He hadn't wept like this in years, since his father's funeral.

"That's all I remember. The next thing I knew, I was back in my truck, a block from my place."

Lamont let the words hang in the air, along with Riley's sobs. Then, in a fatherly tone, he asked, "Mr. Aisling, why didn't you tell the police about this when they first questioned you about your wife's murder?"

Riley took a deep breath. Lamont held his gaze. *Here goes...*

"I couldn't remember, at first. Then it all came back to me. I was afraid they wouldn't believe me, that they would lock me up with crazies."

"Did you think you were crazy?"

"I didn't know what to think at first."

"What changed your mind?"

"Evidence."

Lamont paced slowly before the jury. "Tell us again, where were you the night your wife was killed?"

"I was on an alien ship."

"You spoke of evidence?"

"I began to have flashbacks and dreams from my own memory. They were frightening, but little by little memories began to surface. Of course, now I remember everything. These beings have abducted me before. I have recent marks on my body, but some are years old."

"Marks?"

"Yes, small scars that I don't remember getting. Because they took samples."

"Your Honor," Lamont began, "if I may, I'd like to submit these to the court as evidence," he said, handing over a stack of photographs that showed the various scoop-liked scars covering Riley's body. "Anything else?"

"Yes. There was something implanted in the bridge of my nose."

Lamont held up a plastic baggie. The tiny metal barbell thing was inside. He handed the baggie to the judge, who inspected it with interest.

"Is this what the doctors took out of your nose?"

"Yes."

"What time did you leave your wife that night?"

"A little after four."

This was the home stretch, and Lamont's smile was kind as he asked, "Was Alice Aisling alive when you left her?"

"Yes, sir. I wouldn't hurt my wife. I loved her, even when I hated her. I've wished over and over that I'd stayed with her. Maybe she'd still be alive." He choked back a sob.

"And you can account for your fingerprints at the scene?"

"Yes, we spent the evening together. It's not like I've never been to my sister-in-law's house before. I've been there a million times."

"Why should the jury believe you? Why should they swallow this crazy story about aliens?"

Here was the moment, the line that Lamont had coached him so carefully to deliver. Wiping his eyes, Riley pronounced, "There's more evidence to support my alibi than there is to support my guilt."

"Thank you, Mr. Aisling. You may step down. Your Honor, I wish to call Paul Franklin to the stand.

"Proceed."

A young man with long shaggy hair was sworn in, and slumped into his seat at the witness stand. After he recited a long litany of credentials in a bored voice, Lamont smiled at him.

"Please state for the court, Mr. Franklin, the nature of your work. You can skip the title, because no one here, myself included, will understand it anyway."

Giggles were heard throughout the courtroom.

"I work for the justice department. I'm an analyst. My specialty is identifying metals. I also freelance."

"Have you ever seen this before?" Lamont asked, holding up the barbell.

Franklin's boredom dropped away. "Yes, it was sent to me by Dr. Walker for analysis." His hands went out unconsciously to the barbell.

"And what were you able to determine concerning its origins?"

"It's not a metal. It's not a mineral. To tell you the truth, I can't tell you what it is. Shoot, it ruined my best diamond-head drill. Whatever it is, it's harder than the hardest known substance on earth."

"That's all. Thank you, Mr. Franklin. Your witness."

Keene nodded her head. "I have no questions, Your Honor."

"Fine, then you may step down."

Lamont cleared his throat. He had in his hand the medical report he had read in the restaurant weeks earlier. It was the very report that had reduced his cozy world to the sharp point of a needle. He could only hope it would have the same effect on the jury.

"I would like to call Dr. Walker to the witness stand," Lamont said, gauging the room for a reaction. Jason Walker was well known to the people of the court. It was accepted that he was one of the smartest and most committed doctors in Left Ridge.

"Dr. Walker, three weeks ago, you examined Mr. Aisling. Would you tell the court what you found?"

The young doctor sat back, cool and handsome, and raised a hand. "First, let me say, that when I agreed to examine Mr. Aisling, it was under the assumption that whatever I found, or didn't find, would be reported honestly and openly. I have all the fame and money I could ever need, and at the outset I told Lamont and his staff that I would never lie or disrupt the truth. I am a professional."

"Thank you, Doctor. The people of Left Ridge certainly know you are a man of integrity." Jason Walker's appearance had prompted many smiles around the room; Lamont knew he was scoring big.

"So what did you find?"

"During my initial examination of Mr. Aisling, I found that metal object inside his nasal cavity. Also, I noticed that several of his internal organs were swollen."

"Swollen?"

"Well, that's what I thought initially. As it turned out, they weren't swollen at all—they were misplaced. Turned upside down, sideways, in odd positions at varying degrees."

"Really? And how did you make this determination?"

"I sent the patient for a body scan. Not only were his organs out of place, but his organs were literally covered by scar tissue."

"Uh huh. Wouldn't you develop scar tissue if you had surgery, doctor?"

"Yes, but Mr. Aisling has never undergone surgery outside of a tonsillectomy. He has no evidence of incisions anywhere on his outer body."

Many hushed voices filled the courtroom. Lamont smiled at the sound; it meant he was making waves with this witness.

"Silence, or I'll clear the courtroom," Judge Dempster warned. The bailiff stepped forward menacingly.

Lamont milked the moment. By confronting any questions the jury might ask if they had a chance, he and Jason Walker made a formidable team. "What about an injury? Couldn't that cause the scarring?"

"Well, yes, you could have internal injuries that would cause this kind of scarring, injuries that healed without the aid of surgery. But his scars were so extensive, if they had been the result of an injury, Mr. Aisling wouldn't be here today. He would be dead."

"And these ... misplaced... organs, do they still work? I mean..."

"I know what you mean, Mr. Lamont. Yes, they do. As you can see, Mr. Aisling is still among us, living and breathing."

"So how do you explain this?"

"I can't." These two words were very powerful coming from a man who knew everything, and Lamont knew it. He could see surprise circulating the room, and knew also that Walker was absolutely believed.

"I have no further questions, Your Honor."

"Your witness."

Keene sat quietly for a minute, calculating the odds. She turned her head to look at Riley, then back up at the judge.

"I have no questions, Your Honor."
"Thank you, Doctor. You may step down."

Chapter Seventeen

When the door of the Chameleon Lounge opened and Jake Fry emerged, Hilde snapped herself out of a comfortable doze and murmured, "There you are, you son of a bitch…"

Mike hadn't wanted to leave, but his boss was getting impatient. He was not a cop, he was a reporter, and for the last few days he hadn't reported anything. "Call me if something happens," he'd said, squeezing her hand, and then she'd been alone.

Alone was good. It cleared her mind, made her focus more clearly on the task at hand. Mike had only been gone a few hours when things began to happen.

Almost as if he knew Hilde was nearby in the car, Fry turned his head to stare in her direction. "Maybe somebody tipped him off," Hilde thought, putting one hand on the door handle. There was no way he could have spotted her in the dark, among so many other vehicles.

Fry took a few steps toward her, pulled a handgun from the back of his jeans, and fired.

Gasping, Hilde hit the floor, the gearshift digging painfully into her hip. The bullet hit the windshield with a sharp smack, then whizzed over her head. The maniac had just tried to kill a cop! She grabbed her radio and called for backup.

The handgun blasted again, and another bullet smacked through the windshield; tiny bits of glass rained down into her hair. She couldn't stay in this car like a fish in a barrel.

Keeping low, she put her hand back on the door handle and gave it a tug. The door swung open. She had long ago disconnected the interior light.

Fry called to her, his voice mingling with the thumping music inside the lounge. "Coming out, bitch?" He sounded drunk.

Hilde didn't answer, because that was what he wanted. Instead she reached into her jacket and took her gun from its holster. She could hear Fry's footsteps crunching through the gravel. He fired another shot, this one sailing far wide.

"You come out of there." His voice was much closer, only a few feet from the front of the car.

Only precision timing would save her life. If she left the car too soon, Fry would pick her off with ease. If she stayed too long, he would shoot her where she lay. A plan started to form in her mind; after all, she had only to survive until backup arrived.

She could hear him breathing—it was a harsh, animal sound. He fired another shot, this one into the windshield again, and in that instant Hilde wriggled forward and clicked on the headlights.

Blinded, Fry grunted and swore; Hilde heard the gun hit the gravel. This was her chance. She launched herself through the open door and ran for the Chameleon Lounge, sparing not one second to glance behind her.

Hilde heard Fry swear again, and she heard him stood to pick up the gun.

It was as though Time blinked. In that blink, Hilde saw two possible futures: Fry would aim at her and fire, taking her down. Or, he would aim at her and miss, and she would disappear into the safety of the Lounge.

But there is a third possibility, Hilde thought then: She could whirl around, now, *right now,* and just shoot the bastard.

She was very nearly at the door.

Behind her, the gun was cocked. Fry took aim, fired...

And missed. Hilde ducked and weaved. She put her hand out to grab the door handle. She could hear sirens approaching.

When the gun was cocked again, Hilde spun on her heel and raised her gun. Fry took aim and fired.

Closing arguments began on a bright and clear February day. Lamont seemed optimistic, but warned Riley to expect the worst. "Expecting the best only hurts your heart," he confided as they entered the courtroom.

I know that now, Riley realized inside.

Keene stepped before the jury box, and took a deep intake of air. "On the night of Alice Aisling's murder, Riley Aisling had a fifty-fifty chance of doing the right thing. But the dice were loaded." Keene allowed for a dramatic pause as she gazed at the jury.

"Instead of a confession, instead of even the slightest modicum of remorse, he has concocted this ridiculous alien abduction alibi, complete with evidence that most of us don't even understand. Convenient! Instead of showing remorse, he's acting as though he is the victim!

"Well, he's not the victim, ladies and gentleman. Alice Aisling and her family—they're the victims. And the victimizer is sitting right there before us, and his name is Riley Aisling. Violence begets violence. Mr. Aisling witnessed the murder of his own mother, at his father's hand. This terrible event, in combination with his rage on the night of the murder, turned Aisling into a killing machine.

"He overheard a phone message left for his wife, and he blew up, months of suspicions came to a head. He cursed her, called her a whore, his own wife. A woman he swore to love in sickness and in health, ladies and gentlemen. And Alice was terrified. She screamed and pleaded, until her neighbors, fearing for her safety, summoned the police.

"But there was a storm that night, and the police didn't get there in time. No, they arrived too late to prevent Riley Aisling from bludgeoning and strangling his wife to death.

"We have a responsibility to do the right thing, to deliver justice in the form of a guilty verdict. That is all. Thank you." Shooting a glance Riley's way, Keene returned to her chair. It creaked loudly as she sat.

"Don't worry," Lamont whispered in Riley's ear before rising to launch his customary pace in front of the jury box.

"The prosecution asks you to consider the environment Mr. Aisling grew up in when considering your verdict. Fine. Let's do that. Mr. Aisling was on the run every second of his boyhood. He spent his free time trying to protect his terrified mother from his father. Instead of baseball, he played defense in mind games invented by his despotic father. He learned that avoiding confrontation was the only way to avoid pain." Lamont's voice rose until it rushed around the courtroom like a cold wind. With a rigid finger, he pointed at the prosecutor.

"It's true, Mr. Aisling *did* have a fifty-fifty chance that night, and the dice *were* loaded, but not in the way Ms. Keene would have you believe."

"Throughout his troubled life, Mr. Aisling has sought one thing only—a life of freedom, decency and normalcy. His only mistake was marrying a woman who assured that he would find none of these. Has the State produced one witness—just one voice—who can state that Riley Aisling is anything other than the quiet, gentle, decent man you see before you? Didn't the victim's own sister state flatly that the defendant was incapable of harming his wife? I don't know, ladies and gentlemen, how you feel about alien abduction. I ask only that you keep an open mind. There are things in heaven and on earth that defy explanation. But does that make them less true? Is Riley Aisling a brutal murderer? I'd like to see the evidence, I really would, but there isn't any. Our system of justice is built on evidence…on the preponderance of the evidence. Show me a shred of evidence that points to Mr. Aisling's guilt.

"He called his wife a vile name, yes. He shouted at her. Yes. Does this constitute evidence of a murder? How many of you have cursed your mates, have shouted and yelled. Did you then commit murder?

"Let's examine his alibi. His body bears witness to the ordeal he suffered. His internal organs, ladies and gentlemen—his very internal organs—testify to something that is beyond our understanding. Something happened to Riley Aisling on the night of January 14.

"You heard Dr. Walker, our town's most respected and trusted medical practitioner." Several jurors nodded knowingly.

"You heard the doctor's testimony. Mr. Aisling's organs were not in their proper places, were covered by scar tissue, and yet, the ingenious Dr. Walker himself can't provide any known cause for the enigma. Do you doubt Dr. Walker's professional expertise?"

Several of the jurors shook their heads emphatically. Lamont dropped his voice at last and ceased his pacing to lean on the jury box.

"It all comes down to this," he said firmly, "you can't convict this man if there is a reasonable doubt, and there is nothing but reasonable doubt.

"Look, Riley could have chosen an easier way to present his case, feigned mental illness, or pleaded guilty in exchange for a reduced sentence, but he didn't. He came before you with a difficult story to tell, one that he knew would not be easily believed. But Riley Aisling thought it was important to tell the truth. He did not kill his wife. And based on the preponderance of evidence, you must let him leave this courtroom a free man. Thank you."

Chapter Eighteen

Hilde awoke to pain. Through a haze of hot agony, she could see a tall Asian man in a white coat. The front of the coat was splashed with red.

"She's awake," said someone.

The man leaned over her and lifted her eyelids. "Detective Casey, I'm Doctor Jianguo Zhang. You've been shot in the chest, just below your right shoulder. I know it hurts, but it's not serious. Blink twice if you understand me."

She did. Then she felt very sleepy, so she closed her eyes for a while longer.

Later, when she felt better, she awoke to a deserted hospital room. Her torso was bandaged. Her wound ached, but it was tolerable. Thirsty, she pressed the nurse's call button.

The nurse poured her a glass of cold water from the sink in the bathroom, and Hilde drank it down.

"How are you feeling, Detective?" the nurse asked. Her nametag said "Raimi."

"Much better," Hilde said. She felt weak, and sleepy again, probably from the painkillers. But she had to know what had happened. "Did they get him?"

The nurse sat on the chair at her bedside. "Sort of. They were forced to shoot him."

Hilde closed her eyes. "Damn."

"From what I understand, they had absolutely no alternative. He might still pull through."

"Let's hope so. A confession from him could save an innocent man."

"There's been a guy waiting to see you since you came in. Says he's your boyfriend."

"Is he a big, sloppy, puppy dog type?"

The nurse smiled and blushed. "You said it."

"Send him in."

The wait almost killed Riley, though it was a relatively short one. He felt splintered after three or four hours, but the deliberation stretched to six hours, then ten, then fifteen. The owl had gone days ago from outside his cell, but since a rat had joined him inside, it seemed he was not yet totally alone. Lamont had returned to the office, needing some time to regroup in case of a deadlock.

At 3 in the afternoon on March the third, the police finally came to take him to the courtroom to hear the verdict. A mob had gathered outside, and by the time Riley took a seat in his usual chair next to Lamont, he had absorbed dozens of nasty epithets.

As court was called to order, Alice's parents seated themselves in their accustomed places. The tense, tearful faces were now tainted with fury. Riley swallowed hard.

Please, please, let the jury believe me.

The jury filed back in. One, two, three. *Strangers, all of them.* Strangers would decide his fate.

"Has the jury reached a verdict?"

"We have, your honor."

"How do you find?"

"In the sole count, murder in the first degree..."

Please, please, please...

"We find the defendant, Riley Aisling..."

The courtroom held its breath. There was not a single sound. And then:

"Guilty."

Riley let out his breath in a rush, but there was no time for tears, no time for shock or regrets or horror or help. The courtroom shrank away, the people disappeared, reality imploded. He could hear Junie wailing, could sense the rattle of his own chains as hands closed on his elbows. His mind was numb.

Lamont whispered fiercely in his ear: "This isn't over, kid. Not by a long shot!"

The bailiffs pulled Riley away. Lamont could see it in his face: The moment that verdict was read, it *was* over. Horrified, disillusioned, Riley had given up.

Lamont ignored Keene's infuriatingly smug expression; he knew that he had to keep his cool. Outbursts would not help Riley. Nevertheless, as his client was escorted away, Lamont protested, "Your Honor! I request a new trial on the basis that the jury was not capable of making an unbiased decision."

"Denied," Dempster said. "That is a matter for the Court of Appeals."

"I disagree, Judge."

"Noted, Counselor. Sentencing is set for day after tomorrow. Court is adjourned."

Lamont had not attended a sentencing for four years.

He exited the courtroom and headed for his car, encountering various media along the way. Against their deluge of questions he could erect only a dazed barricade: "We will of course appeal. That's all for now." He knew his brevity surprised them; he had always adored appearing on television.

What would the press think if he told them that this loss made him feel different? His reaction to any rare lost case was inevitably anger and fresh resolve. What if they sensed that at this moment, the great Hagan Lamont was sickened and weak? A few drops of blood in the water would be enough for the press to tear him apart. He could not reveal to them that he felt strangely devastated.

It was not that he doubted his own actions or abilities; those were above reproach. There was no reasonable explanation for the guilty verdict—he had easily proven reasonable doubt and Keene had not met her burden of proof. The explanation was simple, then, if unreasonable: The jury had not been able to accept his evidence.

Lamont got into his car, started it up, and drove slowly home, almost oblivious of other traffic. Was he upset that he had lost? Or was it something more?

He turned down his street, appreciating as always the careful landscaping efforts of his neighbors. April Henry, a mother of four who lived across the street was out at this very moment, planting seeds in her flowerbed. Spring-cleaning fever hung in the air. April waved at him as he pulled into his driveway, and he waved back.

He shut the Lexus down and sat for a moment, listening to the engine cool. In the rearview mirror, he could see the woman across the street working, and suddenly he was struck by a powerful notion:

Every single person in this neighborhood, he thought, and in every other, relies on the System to protect them. Hagan Lamont had always believed in the System and thought that it was an institution to trust and to foster. This afternoon's verdict had caught him completely by surprise; in fact, it had blown his head apart. Why? Because he absolutely knew that his client was innocent, and what was more, he knew he had proved it. But the System said Riley Aisling was guilty.

The System was wrong.

That's why there is a Court of Appeals, he told himself, but his heart sank even further at this thought. There was no reason to believe a second jury would accept the evidence any more readily than the first. There was no reason to trust the System.

What am I going to do? He went to the bar in the living room and was pouring himself a generous brandy when the phone began to ring.

"Hello, Lamont here."

"Hey, Lamont. It's Casey."

"Well, hello. Do you have good news for me, Detective?"

"No. Jake Fry is dead."
The brandy vanished in a gulp.

Chapter Nineteen

The atmosphere in a courtroom during a sentencing is far different than during the actual trial, Lamont thought. A sinking boat has replaced the roller coaster.

Riley Aisling was pale and listless. When Lamont told him of Jake Fry's death, his client sank instantly into a murky depression. Lamont posted guards at Riley's door and had his shoelaces and belt confiscated. This morning an orderly from the hospital had shaved Riley's face for him.

Judge Dempster called the court to order, and it seemed once again that God Himself was looking down on them, a finger raised as if to smite them out of existence with a single gesture. His white brows were drawn sternly over his eyes, casting black shadows on them. "Riley Aisling," he declared, "you have been found guilty of murder in the first degree by a jury of your peers. The District Attorney's office advocates the death penalty."

Riley winced and shrank in his seat. Here it comes, Lamont thought, and could swear he smelled sharp fear oozing from his client's pores.

"There are a number of criteria necessary in arriving at a death sentence, however, that I feel were not met to my satisfaction. The Court will address these matters before a sentence can be handed down."

Lamont found his mouth hanging open and closed it with a snap. At last, a lucky break! In stark contrast to the jury, only the letter of the law influenced Judge Dempster.

"First of all," Dempster continued, "does the evidence show, beyond a reasonable doubt, that there is a likelihood that the defendant will be dangerous in the future? No. There has, in fact, been no evidence presented to show this at all."

"But your Honor..." Keene piped up.

"Quiet, Counselor. Your time is done."

Lamont caught Keene's eye and gave her a dose of her own smug smile.

"Secondly, the defense has presented mitigating circumstances, which must lessen the probability of the jury imposing death. Such circumstances include family problems, the lack of prior criminal record, mental disability, parental abuse, and poverty.

"The Court is convinced that these circumstances have been proven by the defense, and thus rejects the recommendation for the death penalty."

Lamont smiled. It seemed the roller coaster had not been derailed after all. Beside him, his client had begun to sob.

The judge's words had other immediate and powerful effects. The room filled with voices and camera flashes reflected off the ancient polished wood. Mr. And Mrs. Harrison leapt up and fled the courtroom. Even the jury, their faces passive until now, could not restrain themselves from murmuring to each other as they fidgeted in the box. The gavel rose and fell, and all became silent.

"Mr. Aisling," Dempster said. Riley looked up at him, his face wet with tears. Their eyes met, and at that moment, Lamont sensed, judge and convicted were alone in the courtroom. The judge spoke slowly and deliberately; Riley listened intently. "It is the judgment of this court that you be imprisoned in Crestwood Mayne Federal Penitentiary for the rest of your natural life, without the possibility of parole. As the Court has repealed the death penalty, be aware that your automatic appeal is now void. Court is adjourned."

It was odd, Lamont thought, to think of rejoicing at a grim sentence like life imprisonment, yet Riley grinned broadly at him as he was led away by the bailiffs. Then he realized: Imprisonment was nothing new to Riley Aisling. In fact, it was possible that the prospect seemed downright comfortable.

Lamont shivered at the thought. Not for the first time, it occurred to him that Riley might not last very long inside a federal penitentiary. In essence, though the news seemed positive, a life sentence could amount to a death penalty regardless. He doubted the possibility of success, but nevertheless would begin applying for an appeal. The sooner the better; it was a very lengthy process.

Chapter Twenty

Dear Jim and Patty,

    I know that you hate me. I know it makes you happy that I am in a terrible place, with terrible men who are guilty of terrible crimes. If it helps you to say goodbye to Alice, go right ahead and hate me forever, even though I need your forgiveness very much. Not because I am guilty of this crime, but because I never should have married someone as superior as your daughter.

    But you must recognize that I loved her very much. I wanted a future with her; she was the best thing that ever came into my life. Her smile lit up my darkest day. The pain you endure at her loss echoes in my own heart, you must believe me.

    I know I face a lifetime of misery, I have realized this even in the short two months I have spent here. Perhaps I realized it years ago. Life here is very difficult. The other inmates sense that I cannot fight, that violence makes me sick right in the pit of my stomach. They steal my meals and torment me at any opportunity. I tell you this only because I want you to know that I am suffering as much as you are, because that thought too will make you happy.

    But it happened. No matter how much the world rejects or ridicules, I was taken, it happened. This is something that you must face; we are not alone. Hate me if you need to, but know that someday I will be vindicated. I am not crazy, and I am not a liar; they should have believed the alibi.

    Goodbye,
    Riley Aisling

Chapter Twenty-One

Hagan Lamont was beginning to wonder if the justice system was out to get him. Every appeal he had filed had been denied, every single one! Worst of all, when he conveyed this news to his client, Riley never seemed shocked or even disappointed—he seemed resigned.

Every night Lamont had a dream that he himself was a jeweled butterfly, that he floated free and full of joy on clear blue air, only to be netted and imprisoned, wings pinned, and put on display for the amusement of children. Every night around three he awoke, almost insane with the knowledge that an innocent man suffered behind bars and that the System betrayed him on a consistent basis. After only eight months of his life sentence, Riley had lost perhaps forty pounds, obviously slept sparingly, and always sported new bruises whenever Lamont visited, which was about twice a month.

He was not going to last.

What could be done? Lamont had lost his appetite for *Daven's* fine cuisine; it tasted like sand nowadays. His partners had taken the liberty of scheduling appointments for him with Olga Leonard, but he never kept them. They were concerned, Victor told him. They were concerned with his growing obsession. They were concerned for his health and his business. Victor said the publicity surrounding the case had increased their workload tenfold. They needed him. They wanted him to move on.

Move on?

Move on?

How could he move on when the System sneered in his face around every corner? How could he ever trust in anything ever again when, in his heart of hearts, he doubted himself?

Then, one day, everything changed.

Chapter Twenty-Two

It was to be a regular day, a regular visit. Up at three, Lamont backed out of his driveway at four and drove an hour to Crestwood Mayne Federal Penitentiary. He had paperwork with him as always, for Riley to sign, another appeal attempt. Lamont entered the penitentiary, as always, early in the morning, around five, and submitted to frisking, searching, and prodding. Then he sat in the familiar little room that was so like the interrogation room in Left Ridge.

He waited for his client.

He waited.

He waited some more.

Finally, growing annoyed, he rose and knocked on the door. A guard opened it and regarded him expressionlessly.

"I've been waiting for almost an hour. What's the hold up?"

"We can't find your client, Mr. Lamont."

The words hovered in the air a moment before Lamont, stunned, ventured, "What do you mean, you can't find him?"

"He's escaped. We can't find him," the guard repeated. "Please sit down and wait for the warden, sir."

Lamont returned to his seat, sinking slowly onto the hard metal chair. Riley was weak, dispirited, and all alone in here. There were tough-looking guards everywhere; locked doors and steel-plated walls dominated the décor. Despite the prison's first assumption, Lamont knew damn well there was no way his client could have escaped. A tiny spark, starting at the front of his brain somewhere, flared into a ferocious notion in a very short time:

Riley Aisling had been taken again. This time, he had not been returned.

This ferocious notion had cooled to tranquil conviction by the time the warden arrived an hour later. Had he been kept waiting on purpose? There was no way to know, but Lamont let himself dislike the warden anyway.

The warden had very dark skin and bright, even teeth. "Mr. Lamont, so nice to see you again," he said in a velvet tone that implied the exact opposite.

"Mr. West, same here," Lamont said, clasping the warden's hand and shaking it solemnly. "I understand there has been some excitement this morning?"

West nodded. "This morning at five hundred hours, we went to wake Mr. Aisling for roll call. His cell was empty. Your client, Mr. Lamont, has escaped. I want to know if you are aware of anything about how he accomplished this, or where he might have gone."

Lamont couldn't resist a grin. "My client has not escaped. He has been removed."

"Removed? By whom?"

At this Lamont leaned forward, and, with a soft smile and in a soft voice, he said knowingly into West's ear: "Aliens."

West backed off and stared at him. After a moment, he said, "I can see you are unwilling to cooperate. You may go."

"Oh, *may* I?" Lamont gushed. "Thank you *so much!* I truly appreciate your permission, Mr. West. You are not the warden of the world, sir, and I've just realized that I should've left two hours ago."

"I remind you of your obligation to the law should you hear from Aisling."

"You don't need to remind me of any damn thing," Hagan Lamont snapped. "I say this only because my mother brought me up well, and not because I really mean it: Good day, sir."

The drive home was a furious flurry of thoughts and emotions. Would Riley be returned? If so, when? There had to be someone who he could talk to about this…

At least Riley wasn't in that crappy little cell, but he was in the hands of otherworldly beings. Although they had not deliberately injured him in the past, it had to be utterly terrifying. But which was more terrifying: The aliens, or the monsters Riley was locked up with? Was his life now so awful, that even abduction was sweet escape? The idea appalled Lamont. He thought too that only now did he truly comprehend and appreciate the horror of his client's youth. Riley had admitted that he had sometimes been happy to see the big light.

Left Ridge was upon him before he knew it, and almost unconsciously, he turned the wheel in the direction of his office. He knew that there was nothing he could do about Riley's disappearance, and the loss of control he'd felt over all the denied appeals was suddenly magnified into a smothering helplessness.

Helplessness had only one cure: Work.

I'll bury myself up to my eyebrows in work.

There was a Volkswagen bus parked in front of his office. It was painted deepest black and covered with tiny white dots meant to look like stars. The license plate said Zeti –1. Lamont was stunned to realize that Shane Harley was exactly the person he needed to talk to.

Harley was waiting in the big office, drinking coffee and reading Omni. He waited for Lamont to pour himself a cup and sit behind his comfortable old desk. Then he looked up from his magazine and smiled.

"I'm a little psychic," Harley said. "He's gone, isn't he?"

Lamont, unable to be surprised any further in one day, nodded. "Yes."

"His time came. He'll return one day, you know."

"He will?"

"Oh, yes."

"When?"

Shane Harley drained his coffee cup and set it on a corner of Lamont's desk. "Impossible to know. Days. Months. Years. It's up to Them."

Lamont nodded again. He had suddenly decided to take the advice of his partners and talk to Olga Leonard. It *was* time to move on; the case was literally out of his hands. It was time to worry about Hagan Lamont for a while.

When and if Riley were returned, though, he would have to be ready...

Shane Harley smiled, and then rose to go.

"I will be," Hagan Lamont murmured. "I'll be ready."

Dennie Kuhn

Look for these other fine books from JumpNJupiter.com…

TRINITY
By David Bornus

One man. Three stages of Life. A chance to do it all again. While traveling down an unfamiliar road, old Lord Anselm meets two younger versions of himself. Together, these men, from three stages of life, embark on their first exciting adventure together.

CITY AT WORLD'S END
By Ed Reardon

After being catapulted millions of years into the future, the residents of Crestview, Vermont face an impossible choice. These proud New England Yankees must decide between fighting for their freedom, or giving in to the ruling party's demand that they become part of one of the government's alien life exhibits.

THE SWAP
By Alice Wright

Described by syndicated columnist Ernest G. Sloan as "sexy and fast-paced. A real page-turner!" The Swap takes readers on a meteoric voyage through time with two daring men, Mark Peters, a young ex-fighter pilot, and Skylar, a historian from the distant future. After agreeing to trade places for six weeks, the two men find themselves trapped, and are launched on a breathtaking voyage through the present, the future and beyond.

VAL CONE
By Bea Jacques

The Great Drought, which began in the middle of the 22nd Century, A.D., turned the once-fertile earth into a barren desert. At the Reclamation Project, intensive research is underway to speed up reforestation by means of plant cloning. Dr. Val Cone and his beautiful next-in-command, Ela, oversee the operation. When Dr. Seth Hines is released from a mental health facility, Val Cone hires him--a decision he will come to regret. Far from being cured, Dr. Hines sinks deeper into madness as he attempts to clone a super race that will wipe out humanity. Val embarks on a interstellar race against time to find Dr. Hines' lab and destroy his creations.

CHILDREN OF THE PLAGUE
By Kat Hankinson

Editor and reviewer E. Alexander Gerster says Kat Hankinson's debut novel "is an exciting story that brings back the spirit of the Golden Age of science-fiction." The riveting conclusion to Hugo Gernsback's classic serial novel Ralph 124 C41+, the story is set in the year 2700. Earth has been cast into a dark age by a manmade plague. Our only hope for survival is an aging scientist and a young researcher with a terrifying secret locked in her genetic code.

About The Author

Dennie Kuhn is a freelance writer whose work is prominent on the Internet and in print publications like *The Buzz On Exercise and Fitness*. Kuhn lives in Southern Alberta, Canada with her husband and pets, where she is currently working on her next novel. The Alibi is her first long work of fiction.